Tobacco Road

TOBACCO ROAD

Erskine Caldwell

Foreword by Lewis Nordan

Brown Thrasher Books
The University of Georgia Press
Athens and London

Published in 1995 as a Brown Thrasher Book
by the University of Georgia Press, Athens, Georgia 30602
© 1932, 1960 by Erskine Caldwell
Foreword to the Brown Thrasher Edition © 1995
by the University of Georgia Press

The paper in this book meets the guidelines for
permanence and durability of the Committee on
Production Guidelines for Book Longevity of the
Council on Library Resources.

Printed in the United States of America

04 03 02 01 00 P 10 9 8 7 6

Library of Congress Cataloging in Publication Data

Caldwell, Erskine, 1903–
    Tobacco road / Erskine Caldwell ; foreword by Lewis Nordan.
        p. cm.
    "Brown Thrasher Books."
    ISBN 0-8203-1660-1 (alk. paper). — ISBN 0-8203-1661-X (pbk. : alk.
    paper)
    I. Title.
PS3505.A322T6   1995
813'.52—dc20   94-13090

British Library Cataloging in Publication Data available

Tobacco Road was originally published in 1932 by Scribners, New York.
This edition of *Tobacco Road* is reprinted with the permission
of the Beehive Press, Savannah, Georgia, which publishes books about
the history of Georgia.

FOREWORD

Lewis Nordan

W H E N I W A S a boy growing up in the Mississippi Delta in the
1940s, a mule-drawn wagon still trundled through the town in
summer hauling big blocks of ice to homes that were without
refrigerators. Some of my friends' homes were heated in winter
exclusively with wood fires, and cooking was done on an iron
stove fueled by sticks of wood. Chickens scratched about in the
yards. Many homes were without telephones. Water was drawn
in the backyard at an iron pump; the outhouse stood near the
barnyard; in health class at school we learned of the proper posi-
tioning of the outhouse to the water supply. White folks' houses
usually had glass panes in the windows and electricity for a radio
and a single lightbulb or two, not much more. Black folks'
houses were worse, with no windows and lighted by kerosene
lamps, and often drinking water had to be carried in buckets
over long distances. My best friend and his brothers and sisters
and I, when I stayed with them, bathed once a week, one at a
time, in a big zinc washtub on the back porch, while the rest
waited our turn on the other side of the house. Such conditions
were not universal, but they were commonplace.

Yet when we spoke of the poorest, or the most hopeless, or
even the morally reprehensible among us, we said, "They might
as well be living on Tobacco Road." I had never heard the name
of Erskine Caldwell, let alone read one of his books; yet these
words, and this vision of the rural South, had made their way
into the American mind and into our vernacular. Long before I
knew that *Tobacco Road* was a work of fiction, it existed for me as

v

a scrap of fictional geography, vague but real, and I shuddered to imagine its inhabitants.

It is not surprising that a version of Caldwell's world had filtered into the least literary segments of the American consciousness—I mean, into the world of a country schoolboy like me. *Tobacco Road* and *God's Little Acre* were phenomenal successes throughout the world. They sold millions of copies, tens of millions, and were translated into forty-three languages. The greatest critics of the time praised both books. William Faulkner declared Caldwell one of the five best contemporary American writers, along with himself, Hemingway, Fitzgerald, and Dos Passos. Saul Bellow believed Caldwell should have won the Nobel Prize. *Tobacco Road* was made into a successful stage play, running through sixteen hundred performances, and a Hollywood movie, produced by Daryl Zanuck and directed by John Ford, complete with a happy ending (which Caldwell himself found appalling). *God's Little Acre* was banned in Boston and became the subject of a celebrated obscenity trial in which the author was vindicated in the New York courts. In perhaps the unkindest cut of all, *God's Little Acre* was also banned in Caldwell's native state of Georgia. Virtually no one in this country had not heard of these two books. And almost everyone had formed an opinion not only of the books and their author but of the South as well. When we accused others of living on Tobacco Road, we were distancing ourselves from a sociological stratum of society that we were afraid of being associated with, for that is how we— or I, anyway—understood *Tobacco Road*, as a sociological statement about a region.

In important ways the books were indeed sociological. On one level, *Tobacco Road* deals with dirt-poor sharecroppers exploited by the rich. Jeeter Lester borrows money from the loan companies that then begin to tell him how to plant his cotton, how much guano to use per acre. When Jeeter can't pay the interest on the loan, it is added to the principal, and he is charged interest on that too. At the harvest Jeeter has paid back nearly double his loan, and his share of the crop comes to only seven dollars.

"Seven dollars for a year's labor did not seem to him a fair portion of the proceeds from the cotton, especially as he had done all the work, and had furnished the land and the mule, too." Jeeter's tragedy, and that of many others like him, is that he had once owned this land but had it wrested away by high taxes and creditors all too ready to foreclose on a mortgage. When Jeeter realizes he has had to hire the mule for ten dollars, he calculates the year's work as a three dollar loss. There is a sadness, even a tragedy, at the core of these lives that seem as sterile as the land on which they are lived. The degradation and oppression end only in violent death.

Likewise, *God's Little Acre* deals with a family of poor whites whose lives have been spiritually attached to the soil but whom now the farms can no longer support. Whereas the Lesters had managed (foolishly, perhaps) not to capitulate to the new economy and take jobs in town, the characters of *God's Little Acre* have been forced to take work in the textile mills. At the heart of the book is a struggle between the owners of the mills and the labor union, which has gone on strike for better conditions and wages. At the climax of the book, Will Thompson, a cotton weaver in a Carolina mill, dies a hero's death in a dramatic attempt to reopen the mill. Other violent deaths, both murder and suicide, follow. Griselda speaks the hopeless message of these characters' lives as she holds her husband Buck in her arms: "There was a mean trick played on us somewhere. God put us in the bodies of animals and tried to make us act like people." And Ty Ty Walden looks at the land where so many have died: "The farm before him looked desolate. The piles of red clay and yellow sand, the wide red craters between, the red soil without vegetation." This is an emblem of the internal world of Ty Ty as well as of his external world.

These are despairing moments. And yet these novels seem much richer than even these important themes can reveal. Sometimes the writing veers from the hard naturalism and realistic dialogue, which Caldwell is so skilled at creating, into pure poetry. Sentences leap off the page by virtue of their perfect simplicity of observation and expression. A character says, "Once the sun was so hot a bird came down and walked beside me in my shadows." And there is this passage of prose-poetry:

The men who worked in the mill looked tired and worn, but the girls were in love with the looms and the spindles and the flying lint. The wild-eyed girls on the inside of the ivy-walled cotton mills . . . with eyes like morning glories, and the men stood on the hot streets looking at each other while they spat their lungs into the deep yellow dust. . . .

And I love the comedy of *God's Little Acre* and *Tobacco Road*. Despite the despair and the violence, these novels are, in some ways, essentially comic. I love Ty Ty Walden's compulsive devotion to digging for gold on farmland. I will never forget my feeling as a teenager as I watched Jeeter Lester eat that croker sack of raw turnips; it was the most amazing thing I had ever seen on a page. I felt the same way as I watched the old grandmother get run over flat by Dude's new car and the casual indifference of her family who watch her die. It is dark comedy, to be sure, in the tradition of Twain and Faulkner, and central to Caldwell's complex vision.

Complexity of vision seems to me the key to this writer's genius. He was political, sociological, poetic, spiritual, comic, even grotesque, and there is a raw lustiness in many of the scenes. Yet none of this quite describes Caldwell for me. It is the narrative energy that seems most remarkable and lasting. On page 1 he begins his tale—with turnips or gold diggers, it doesn't matter—and we are swept along a road that is both familiar and surprising, until we come to its unhappy end. The trails we follow and the people we meet seem utterly original, yet somehow a part of the world we live in. And despite the despair of his message, his characters seem created out of love rather than anger, not mere pawns in a sermon against injustice but warm-blooded, real people living out lives in a certain joy despite the severity of their limitations. In *Tobacco Road* and *God's Little Acre*, Caldwell is a storyteller. He tells us about people with hearts that can be

viii

broken, or with hearts that have broken so often these people feel nothing. All the rest is a function of the tales he tells.

When I was a boy, living on that dusty road in the Mississippi Delta a long time ago, and first read the novels of Erskine Caldwell, I felt as if I were looking through a keyhole into a world that I had observed each day and yet had never seen. Rereading them, I have seen and recognized it again, and again I am utterly surprised.

Tobacco Road

CHAPTER I

Lov Bensey trudged homeward through the deep white sand of the gully-washed tobacco road with a sack of winter turnips on his back. He had put himself to a lot of trouble to get the turnips; it was a long and tiresome walk all the way to Fuller and back again.

The day before, Lov had heard that a man over there was selling winter turnips for fifty cents a bushel, so he had started out with half a dollar early that morning to buy some. He had already walked seven and a half miles, and it was a mile and a half yet back to his house at the coal chute.

Four or five of the Lesters were standing in the yard looking at Lov when he put his sack down and stopped in front of the house. They had been watching Lov ever since he was first seen an hour before on the sand hill nearly two miles away, and now that he was actually within reach, they were prepared to stop him from carrying the turnips any farther.

Lov had his wife to feed and provide for, in addition to himself, and he was careful not to allow any of the Lesters to come too close to the sack of turnips. Usually when he came by the Lester place with turnips or sweet potatoes, or for that matter with any kind of food, he left the road half a mile from the house and made a wide circle through the fields, returning to the road a safe distance beyond. To-day, though, he had to speak to Jeeter about something of great importance, and he had ventured closer to the house than he had ever done before when carrying home turnips or sweet potatoes.

Lov's wife was Jeeter Lester's youngest daughter, Pearl. She was only twelve years old the summer before when he had married her.

The Lesters watched Lov closely while he stood in the middle of the road. He had dropped the sack from his shoulder, but he held the neck of it in the rigid grasp of both hands. No one in the yard had changed his position during the past ten minutes. The next move was left entirely up to Lov.

When Lov came to the house and stopped, he had a good reason for doing so; otherwise he would never have come within hailing distance. He wanted to speak to Jeeter about Pearl.

Pearl would not talk. She would not say a word, no matter how persuasive Lov tried to be, nor how angry he was; she even hid from Lov when he came home from the coal chute, and when he found her, she slipped away from his grasp and ran off into the broom-sedge out of sight. Sometimes she would even stay in the broom-sedge all night, remaining out there until Lov went to work the next morning.

Pearl had never talked, for that matter. Not because she could not, but simply because she did not want to. When she was at home, before Lov had married her, she had stayed apart from the other Lesters and rarely opened her mouth from the beginning of one day to the next. Only her mother, Ada, had been able to converse with her, and even then Pearl had never used more than the barest of negatives and affirmatives in reply. But Ada was herself like that. She had begun to talk voluntarily only during the past ten years. Before then, Jeeter

2

had had the same trouble with her that Lov was now having with Pearl.

Lov asked Pearl questions, he kicked her, he poured water over her, he threw rocks and sticks at her, and he did everything else he could think of that he thought might make her talk to him. She cried a lot, especially when she was seriously hurt, but Lov did not consider that as conversation. He wanted her to ask him if his back were sore, and when was he going to get his hair cut, and when was it going to rain again. But Pearl would not say anything.

He had spoken to Jeeter several times before about his troubles with Pearl, but Jeeter did not know what was the matter with her. Ever since she was a baby she had been like that, he said; and Ada had remained untalkative until the last few years. What Jeeter had not been able to break down in Ada for forty years, hunger had. Hunger loosened her tongue, and she had been complaining ever since. Jeeter did not attempt to recommend the starving of Pearl, because he knew she would go somewhere to beg food, and would get it.

"Sometimes I think it's just the old devil in her," Lov had said several times. "To my way of thinking, she ain't got a scratch of religion in her. She's going to hell-fire when she dies, sure as day comes."

"Now, maybe she ain't pleased with her married life," Jeeter had suggested. "Maybe she ain't satisfied with what you provide her with."

"I done everything I can think of to make her satisfied and contented. Every week I go to Fuller on pay-day and buy her a pretty. I get her snuff, but she won't take none; I get her a little piece of calico, but she won't sew it. Looks like she wants something I ain't got and can't get her. I wish I knowed what it was. She's such a pretty little girl—all them long yellow curls hanging down her back sort of gets me all crazy sometimes. I don't know what's

3

going to happen to me. I've got the need of Pearl for a wife as bad as any man ever had."

"I expect she's too young yet to appreciate things," Jeeter had said. "She ain't grown up yet like Ellie May and Lizzie Belle and Clara and the other gals. Pearl ain't nothing but a little gal yet. She don't even look like a woman, so far."

"If I had knowed she was going to be like she is, maybe I wouldn't have wanted to marry her so bad. I could have married me a woman what wants to be married to me. But I don't want Pearl to go now, though. I sort of got used to her around, and I'd sure miss seeing them long yellow curls hanging down her back. They make a man feel kind of lonesome some way. She sure is a pretty little girl, no matter if she does act like she does all the time."

Lov had gone back home that time and told Pearl what Jeeter said about her, but she sat in the chair and made no sign of answering him. Lov did not know what to do about her after that. But he had realized from that time on that she was still a little girl. During the eight months they had been married she had grown three or four inches in height, and she weighed about fifteen pounds more now than she had at the beginning. She still did not weigh much more than a hundred pounds, though she was gaining in weight and height every day.

What Lov wanted to speak to Jeeter about now in particular was the way Pearl had of refusing to sleep with him. They had been married almost a year, and still she slept by herself, as she had done since the first. She slept by herself on a pallet on the floor, refusing even to let Lov kiss her or touch her in any way. Lov had told her that cows were not any good until they had been freshened, and that the reason he married her was because he wanted to kiss her and feel her long yellow curls and sleep with her; but Pearl had not even indicated that she

4

heard him or knew what he was talking about. Next to wanting to kiss her and talk to her, Lov wanted to see her eyes. Yet even this pleasure she denied him; her pale blue eyes were always looking off into another direction when he came and stood in front of her.

Lov still stood in the middle of the road looking at Jeeter and the other Lesters in the yard. They were waiting for him to make the first move; friendly or hostile, it mattered little to them so long as there were turnips in the sack.

Jeeter was wondering where Lov had got the turnips. It did not occur to him that Lov had bought them with money; Jeeter had long before come to the conclusion that the only possible way a quantity of food could be obtained was by theft. But he had not been able to locate a turnip patch that year anywhere within five or six miles. There had been planted a two-acre field the year before over at the Peabody place, but the Peabody men had kept people out of the field with shotguns then, and this year they had not even planted turnips.

"Why don't you come in the yard off the tobacco road, Lov?" Jeeter said. "Ain't no sense standing out there. Come in and rest yourself."

Lov made no reply, nor did he move. He was debating within himself the danger of entering the yard, against the safety of staying where he was in the road.

For the past few weeks Lov had been thinking about taking some plow-lines and tying Pearl in the bed at night. He had tried everything that he could think of so far, except force, and he was still determined to make her act as he thought a wife should. He had reached the point now where he wanted Jeeter's advice before going ahead with the plan. He believed Jeeter would know whether it was advisable from the practical side, since Jeeter had had to contend with Ada for almost a lifetime. He knew Ada had once acted as Pearl was now doing, but Jeeter

5

had not been treated as he was treated, because Ada had borne him seventeen children, while Pearl had not even begun to have the first one.

If Jeeter said it would be satisfactory to tie Pearl in bed, then he would go ahead and do it. Jeeter knew more about such things than he did. Jeeter had been married to Ada forty years.

Lov hoped that Jeeter would offer to go down to the house at the coal chute and help him tie Pearl in the bed. Pearl fought back so fiercely whenever he attempted to catch her that he was afraid he would not be able to accomplish anything without Jeeter's help.

The Lesters stood around in the yard and on the front porch waiting to see what Lov was going to do next. There had been very little in the house again that day to eat; some salty soup Ada had made by boiling several fatback rinds in a pan of water, and corn bread, was all there was when they had sat down to eat. There had not been enough to go around even then, and the old grandmother had been shoved out of the kitchen when she tried to come inside.

Ellie May stood behind a chinaberry tree, looking around the trunk at Lov. She moved her head from one side of the tree to the other, trying to attract Lov's attention.

Ellie May and Dude were the only Lester children left at home. All the others had gone away and married, some of them just leaving in a casual way as though they were only walking down to the coal chute to see the freight trains. When they failed to return within two or three days, it was known that they had left home.

Dude was throwing a lopsided baseball at the side of the house, and catching it on the rebound. The ball hit the house like a clap of thunder, rattling the loose weather-boarding until the vibration swayed the house from side to side. He threw the ball continually, the ball

6

bounding with unfailing regularity back across the sandy yard to where he stood.

The three-room house sat precariously on stacks of thin lime-rock chips that had been placed under the four corners. The stones had been laid one on top of the other, the beams spiked, and the house nailed together. The ease and simplicity with which it had been built was now evident. The centre of the building sagged between the sills; the front porch had sagged loose from the house, and was now a foot or more lower than it originally was; and the roof sagged in the centre where the supporting rafters had been carelessly put together. Most of the shingles had rotted, and after every wind-storm pieces of them were scattered in all directions about the yard. When the roof leaked, the Lesters moved from one corner of the room to another, their movements finally outlasting the duration of the rain. The house had never been painted.

Jeeter was trying to patch a rotten inner-tube. He had said that if he could ever get all the tires on the old automobile standing up at the same time again, he would haul a load of wood to Augusta and sell it. Woodcutters were being paid two dollars a load for seasoned pine delivered in the city; but the blackjack that Jeeter tried to make people buy for fuel never brought him more than fifty or seventy-five cents. Usually, when he did succeed in getting a load of it to Augusta, he was not able to give it away; nobody, it seemed, was foolish enough to buy wood that was tougher than iron water-pipes. People argued with Jeeter about his mule-like determination to sell blackjack for fuel, and they tried to convince him that as firewood it was practically worthless; but Jeeter said he wanted to clear the land of the scrub oak because he was getting ready to farm it again.

Lov had by that time moved a few steps nearer the yard and had sat down in the tobacco road with his feet in the drain ditch. He kept one hand gripped tightly

7

around the mouth of the sack where it had been tied together with a piece of twine.

Ellie May continued to peer from behind the chinaberry tree, trying to attract Lov's attention. Each time he glanced in that direction, she jerked her head back so he could not see her.

"What you got in that there croker sack, Lov?" Jeeter shouted across the yard. "I been seeing you come a far piece off with that there croker sack on your back. I sure would like to know what you got on the inside of it. I heard it said that some people has got turnips this year."

Lov tightened his grip on the mouth of the sack, looking from Jeeter to the next Lester in turn. He saw Ellie May peering at him from behind the chinaberry tree.

"Did you have a hard time getting what you got there in the sack, Lov?" Jeeter said. "You look like you is all out of breath."

"I want to say something to you, Jeeter," he said. "It's about Pearl."

"What's that gal done now, Lov? Is she treating you mean some more?"

"It's just like she's always done, only I'm getting pretty durn tired of it by this time. I don't like the way she acts. I never did take to the way she does, but it's getting worse and worse all the time. All the niggers make fun of me because of the way she treats me."

"Pearl is just like her Ma," Jeeter said. "Her Ma used to do the queerest things in her time."

"Every time I want to have her around me, she runs off and won't come back when I call her. Now, what I say is, what in hell is the sense in me marrying a wife if I don't get none of the benefits. God didn't intend for it to be that way. He don't want a man to be treated like that. It's all right for a woman to sort of tease a man into doing what she wants done, but Pearl don't seem to be aiming after that. She ain't teasing me, to her way of thinking,

8

but it sure does act that way on me. Right now I feel like I want a woman what ain't so ———"

"What you got in that there croker sack, Lov?" Jeeter said. "I been seeing you for the past hour or longer, ever since you came over the top of that far hill yonder."

"Turnips, by God," Lov said, looking at the Lester women.

"Where'd you get turnips, Lov?"

"Wouldn't you like to know!"

"I was thinking maybe we might fix up some sort of a trade, Lov—me and you. Now, I could go down to your house and sort of tell Pearl she's got to sleep in the bed with you. That's what you was aiming to speak to me about, wasn't it? You want her to sleep in the bed, don't you?"

"She ain't never slept in the bed. It's that durn pallet on the floor that she sleeps on every night. Reckon you could make her stop doing that, Jeeter?"

"I'd be pleased something powerful to make her do what she ain't doing. That is, if me and you could make a trade with them turnips, Lov."

"That's what I came by here for—to speak to you about Pearl. But I ain't going to let you have none of these turnips, though. I had to pay fifty cents for this many in a sack, and I had to walk all the way to the other side of Fuller and back to fetch them. You're Pearl's daddy, and you ought to make her behave for nothing. She don't pay no attention to nothing I tell her to do."

"By God and by Jesus, Lov, all the damn-blasted turnips I raised this year is wormy. And I ain't had a good turnip since a year ago this spring. All my turnips has got them damn-blasted green-gutted worms in them, Lov. What God made turnip-worms for, I can't make out. It appears to me like He just naturally has got it in good and heavy for a poor man. I worked all the fall last year digging up a patch of ground to grow turnips in, and then when they're getting about big enough to pull up and eat,

9

along comes these damn-blasted green-gutted turnip-worms and bore clear to the middle of them. God is got it in good and heavy for the poor. But I ain't complaining, Lov. I say, 'The good Lord knows best about turnips.' Some of these days He'll bust loose with a heap of bounty and all us poor folks will have all we want to eat and plenty to clothe us with. It can't always keep getting worse and worse every year like it has got since the big war. God, He'll put a stop to it some of these days and make the rich give back all they've took from us poor folks. God is going to treat us right. He ain't going to let it keep on like it is now. But we got to stop cussing Him when we ain't got nothing to eat. He'll send a man to hell and the devil for persisting in doing that."

Lov dragged the sack of turnips across the drain ditch and sat down again. Jeeter laid aside the rotten inner-tube and waited.

CHAPTER II

Lov opened the sack, selected a large turnip, wiping it clean with his hands, and took three big bites one after the other. The Lester women stood in the yard and on the porch looking at Lov eat. Ellie May came from behind the chinaberry tree and sat down not far from Lov on a pine stump. Ada and the old grandmother were on the porch watching the turnip in Lov's hand become smaller and smaller with each bite.

"Now, if Pearl was anything like Ellie May, she wouldn't act like she does," Lov said. "I'd have taken Ellie May at the start if it wasn't for that face of hers. But I knowed I couldn't sleep with no peace of mind at night with her in the bed with me, and knowing how it looked in the daylight. Pearl looks pretty, and she's a right smart piece to want to sleep with, but I just can't make her stay off of that durn pallet on the floor when night comes. You got to come down there and make her do like she ought to act, Jeeter. I been married to her near on to a whole year, and all that time I could just as well been shovelling coal at the chute night and day without ever going to my house. That ain't the way it was intended for it to be. A man has the right to want his wife to get in the bed when dark comes. I ain't never heard of a woman wanting to sleep on a durn pallet on the floor every night in the whole year. Pearl is queer that way."

"By God and by Jesus, Dude," Jeeter said, "ain't you never going to stop bouncing that there ball against that there old house? You've clear about got all the weatherboards knocked off already. The durned old house is going to pitch over and fall on the ground some of these days if you don't stop doing that."

Jeeter picked up the inner-tube again, and tried to make the patch stick to the rubber. The old automobile against which he was sitting was the last of his possessions. The year before, the cow had died, leaving him with the car. Up until that time he had had a way of boasting about his goods, but when the cow went, he did not even mention the car any more. He had begun to think that he was indeed a poor man. No longer was there anything he could mortgage when the time came each spring to buy seed-cotton and guano; the automobile had been turned down at the junk yard in Augusta. But he still had wood to sell; it was the wiry blackjack that grew behind the house. He was trying now to patch the inner-tube so he could haul a load of it to Augusta some time that week. Ada said all the meal was gone, and the meat, too. They had been living off of fat-back rinds several days already, and after they were gone, there would be nothing for them to eat. A load of blackjack would bring fifty or seventy-five cents in Augusta, if he could find a man who would buy it. When the old cow had died, Jeeter hauled the carcass to the fertilizer plant in Augusta and received two dollars and a quarter for it. After that, there was nothing left to sell but blackjack.

"Quit chunking that durn ball at them there weatherboards, Dude," he said. "You don't never stop doing what I tell you. That ain't no way to treat your old Pa, Dude. You ought to sort of help me out, instead of always doing something contrary."

"Aw, go to hell, you old dried-up clod," Dude said, throwing the ball at the side of the house with all his

12

might and scooping up a fast grounder on the rebound. "Nobody asked you nothing."

The old grandmother, Jeeter's mother, crawled under the front porch for the old burlap sack, and went across the tobacco road towards the grove for some dead twigs. No one paid any attention to her.

Wood for the kitchen stove and fireplace was never cut and hauled to the house; Jeeter would not do it, and he could not make Dude do that kind of work. Old Mother Lester knew there was no food for them to cook, and that it would be a waste of time for her to go after the dead twigs and make a fire in the cook-stove; but she was hungry, and she was always hoping that God would provide for them if she made a fire in the kitchen at meal-time. Knowing that there were turnips in Lov's sack made her frantic with hunger. She could sometimes stand the pain of it in her stomach when she knew there was nothing to eat, but when Lov stood in full view taking turnips out of the sack, she could not bear the sight of seeing food no one would let her have.

She hobbled across the road and over the old cotton field that had not been planted and cultivated in six or seven years. The field had grown up in broom-sedge at the start, and now the gnarled and sharp stubs of a new blackjack growth were beginning to cover the ground. She tripped and fell several times on her way to the grove of trees, and her clothes had been torn so many times before that the new tears in the skirt and jacket could not be distinguished from the older ones. The coat and shirt she wore had been torn into strips and shreds by the briars and blackjack pricks in the thicket where she gathered up the dead twigs for fire-wood, and there never had been new clothes for her. Hobbling through the brown broom-sedge, she looked like an old scarecrow, in her black rags.

The February wind whistled through the strips of black cloth, whirling them about in the air until it looked

13

as if she were shaking violently with palsy. Her stockings had been made by wrapping some of the longer of the black rags around her legs and tying the ends with knots. Her shoes were pieces of horse-collars cut into squares and tied around her feet with strings. She went after the dead twigs morning, noon, and night; when she returned to the house each time, she made a fire in the cook-stove and sat down to wait.

Ada shifted the snuff stick to the other side of her mouth and looked longingly at Lov and his sack of turnips. She held the loose calico dress over her chest to keep out the cool February wind blowing under the roof of the porch. Every one else was sitting or standing in the sunshine.

Ellie May got down from the pine stump and sat on the ground. She moved closer and closer to Lov, sliding herself over the hard white sand.

"Is you in mind to make a trade with them turnips?" Jeeter asked Lov. "I'm wanting turnips, God Himself only knows how bad."

"I ain't trading turnips to nobody," he said.

"Now, Lov, that ain't no way to talk. I ain't had a good turnip since a year ago this spring. All the turnips I've et has got them damn-blasted green-gutted worms in them. I sure would like to have some good turnips right now. Wormy ones like mine was ain't fit for a human."

"Go over to Fuller and buy yourself some, then," he said, eating the last of his fourth turnip. "I went over there to get mine."

"Now, Lov, ain't I always been good to you? That ain't no way for you to talk. You know I ain't got a penny to my name and no knowing where to get money. You got a good job and it pays you a heap of money. You ought to make a trade with me so I'll have something to eat and won't have to starve to death. You don't want to sit there and see me starve, do you, Lov?"

14

"I don't make but a dollar a day at the chute. House-rent takes up near about all of that, and eating, the rest of it."

"Makes no difference, Lov. I ain't got a penny to my name, and you is."

"I can't help that. The Lord looks at us with equal favor, they say. He gives me mine, and if you don't get yours, you better go talk to Him about it. It ain't none of my troubles. I've got plenty of my own to worry about. Pearl won't never ——"

"Ain't you never going to stop chunking that durn ball against the house, Dude?" Jeeter shouted. "That noise near about splits my poor head wide open."

Dude slammed the baseball against the loose weather-boards with all his might. Pieces of splintered pine fell over the yard, and rotten chunks dropped to the ground beside the house. Dude threw the ball harder each time, it seemed, and several times the ball almost went through the thin walls of the house.

"Why don't you go somewheres and steal a sack of tur-nips?" Dude said. "You ain't fit for nothing else no more. You sit around here and cuss all the time about not hav-ing nothing to eat, and no turnips—why don't you go somewheres and steal yourself something? God ain't going to bring you nothing. He ain't going to drop no turnips down out of the sky. He ain't got no time to be wasted on fooling with you. If you wasn't so durn lazy you'd do something instead of cuss about it all the time."

"My children all blame me because God sees fit to make me poverty-ridden, Lov," Jeeter said. "They and Ma is all the time cussing me because we ain't got noth-ing to eat. I ain't had nothing to do with it. It ain't my fault that Captain John shut down on giving us rations and snuff. It's his fault, Lov. I worked all my life for Cap-tain John. I worked harder than any four of his niggers in the fields; then the first thing I knowed, he came down

15

here one morning and says he can't be letting me be getting no more rations and snuff at the store. After that he sells all the mules and goes up to Augusta to live. I can't make no money, because there ain't nobody wanting work done. Nobody is taking on share-croppers, neither. Ain't no kind of work I can find to do for hire. I can't even raise me a crop of my own, because I ain't got no mule in the first place, and besides that, won't nobody let me have seed-cotton and guano on credit. Now I can't get no snuff and rations, excepting once in a while when I haul a load of wood up to Augusta. Captain John told the merchants in Fuller not to let me have no more snuff and rations on his credit, and I don't know where to get nothing. I'd raise a crop of my own on this land if I could get somebody to sign my guano-notes, but won't nobody do that for me, neither. That's what I'm wanting to do powerful strong right now. When the winter goes, and when it gets to be time to burn off broom-sedge in the fields and underbrush in the thickets, I sort of want to cry, I reckon it is. The smell of that sedge-smoke this time of year near about drives me crazy. Then pretty soon all the other farmers start plowing. That's what gets under my skin the worse. When the smell of that new earth turning over behind the plows strikes me, I get all weak and shaky. It's in my blood—burning broom-sedge and plowing in the ground this time of year. I did it for near about fifty years, and my Pa and his Pa before him was the same kind of men. Us Lesters sure like to stir the earth and make plants grow in it. I can't move off to the cotton mills like the rest of them do. The land has got a powerful hold on me.

"This raft of women and children is all the time bellowing for snuff and rations, too. It don't make no difference that I ain't got nothing to buy it with—they want it just the same. I reckon, Lov, I'll just have to wait for the good Lord to provide. They tell me He takes care of His people, and I'm waiting for Him to take some notice of me. I don't reckon there's another man between here and Augusta who's as bad off as I is. And down the other way, neither, between here and McCoy. It looks like everybody has got goods and credit excepting me. I don't know why that is, because I always give the good Lord His due. Him and me has always been fair and square with each other. It's time for Him to take some notice of the fix I'm in. I don't know nothing else to do, except wait for Him to take notice. It don't do me no good to try to beg snuff and rations, because ain't nobody going to give it to me. I've tried all over this part of the country, but don't nobody pay no attention to my requests. They say they ain't got nothing neither, but I can't see how that is. It don't look like everybody ought to be poverty-ridden just because they live on the land instead of going to the mills. If I've been a sinful man, I don't know what it is I've done. I don't seem to remember anything I done powerful sinful. It didn't used to be like it is now, either. I can recall a short time back when all the merchants in Fuller was tickled to give me credit, and I always had plenty of money to spend then, too. Cotton was selling upwards of thirty cents a pound, and nobody came around to collect debts. Then all of a sudden the merchants in Fuller wouldn't let me have no more goods on time, and pretty soon the sheriff comes and takes away near about every durn piece of goods I possessed. He took every durn thing I had, excepting that old automobile and the cow. He said the cow wasn't no good, because she wouldn't take no freshening, and the automobile tires was all wore out.

"And now I can't get no credit, I can't hire out for pay, and nobody wants to take on share-croppers. If the good Lord don't start bringing me help pretty soon, it will be too late to help me with my troubles."

Jeeter paused to see if Lov were listening. Lov had his

17

head turned in another direction. He was looking at Ellie May now. She had at last got him to give her some attention.

Ellie May was edging closer and closer to Lov. She was moving across the yard by raising her weight on her hands and feet and sliding herself over the hard white sand. She was smiling at Lov, and trying to make him take more notice of her. She could not wait any longer for him to come to her, so she was going to him. Her harelip was spread open across her upper teeth, making her mouth appear as though she had no upper lip at all. Men usually would have nothing to do with Ellie May; but she was eighteen now, and she was beginning to discover that it should be possible for her to get a man in spite of her appearance.

"Ellie May's acting like your old hound used to do when he got the itch," Dude said to Jeeter. "Look at her scrape her bottom on the sand. That old hound used to make the same kind of sound Ellie May's making, too. It sounds just like a little pig squealing, don't it?"

"By God and by Jesus, Lov, I want some good eating turnips," Jeeter said. "I ain't et nothing all winter but meal and fat-back, and I'm wanting turnips something powerful. All the ones I raised has got them damn-blasted green-gutted worms in them. Where's you get them turnips at anyhow, Lov? Maybe we could make a trade of some kind or another. I always treated you fair and square. You ought to give them to me, seeing as I ain't got none. I'll go down to your house the first thing in the morning and tell Pearl she's got to stop acting like she does. It's a durn shame for a gal to do the way she's treating you—I'll tell her she's got to let you have your rights with her. I never heard of a durn gal sleeping on a pallet on the floor when her husband has got a bed for her, nohow. Pearl won't keep that up after I tell her about it. That ain't no way to treat a man when he's gone to the

18

bother of marrying. It's time she was knowing it, too. I'll go down there the first thing in the morning and tell her to get in the bed."

Lov was paying no attention to Jeeter now. He was watching Ellie May slide across the yard towards him. When she came a little closer, he reached in the sack and took out another turnip, and began taking big bites out of it. He did not bother to wipe the sand from it this time.

Ada shifted the snuff stick to the other side of her mouth again, and watched Ellie May and Lov with gaping jaw.

Dude stood watching Ellie May, too.

"Ellie May's going to get herself full of sand if she don't stop doing that," Dude said. "Your old hound used never to keep it up that long at a time. He didn't squeal all the time neither, like she's doing."

"By God and by Jesus, Lov," Jeeter said, "I'm wanting turnips. I could come near about chewing up a whole croker sack full between now and bedtime to-night."

CHAPTER III

JEETER's reiterated and insistent plea for turnips was having less and less effect upon Lov. He was not aware that any one was talking to him. He was interested only in Ellie May now.

"Ellie May's straining for Lov, ain't she?" Dude said, nudging Jeeter with his foot. "She's liable to bust a gut if she don't look out."

The inner-tube Jeeter was attempting to patch again was on the verge of falling into pieces. The tires themselves were in a condition even more rotten. And the Ford car, fourteen years old that year, appeared as if it would never stand together long enough for Jeeter to put the tire back on the wheel, much less last until it could be loaded with blackjack for a trip to Augusta. The touring-car's top had been missing for seven or eight years, and the one remaining fender was linked to the body with a piece of rusty baling wire. All the springs and horsehair had disappeared from the upholstery; the children had taken the seats apart to find out what was on the inside, and nobody had made an attempt to put them together again.

The appearance of the automobile had not been improved by the dropping off of the radiator in the road somewhere several years before, and a rusty lard-can with a hole punched in the bottom was wired to the water pipe on top of the engine in its place. The lard-can failed to fill the need for a radiator, but it was much better than nothing. When Jeeter got ready to go somewhere, he filled the lard pail to overflowing, jumped in, and drove until the water splashed out and the engine locked up with heat. He would get out then and look for a creek so he could fill the pail again. The whole car was like that. Chickens had roosted on it, when there were chickens at the Lesters' to roost, and it was speckled like a guinea-hen. Now that there were no chickens on the place, no one had ever taken the trouble to wash it off. Jeeter had never thought of doing such a thing, and neither had any of the others.

Ellie May had dragged herself from one end of the yard to the opposite side. She was now within reach of Lov where he sat by his sack of turnips. She was bolder, too, than she had ever been before, and she had Lov looking at her and undisturbed by the sight of her harelip. Ellie May's upper lip had an opening a quarter of an inch wide that divided one side of her mouth into unequal parts; the slit came to an abrupt end almost under her left nostril. The upper gum was low, and because her gums were always fiery red, the opening in her lip made her look as if her mouth were bleeding profusely. Jeeter had been saying for fifteen years that he was going to have Ellie May's lip sewed together, but he had not yet got around to doing it.

Dude picked up a piece of rotted weatherboard that had been knocked from the house and threw it at his father. He did not take his gaze from Ellie May and Lov, however. Their actions, and Ellie May's behavior, held him spellbound.

"What you want now, Dude?" Jeeter said. "What's the matter with you—chunking weatherboarding at me like that?"

"Ellie May's horsing," Dude said.

Jeeter glanced across the yard where Lov and Ellie May were sitting close together. The trunk of a chinaberry tree partly obscured his view of all that was taking place, but he could see that she was sitting on Lov's outstretched legs, astride his knees, and that he was offering her a turnip from the sack beside him.

"Ellie May's horsing, ain't she, Pa?" Dude said.

"I reckon I done the wrong thing by marrying Pearl to Lov," Jeeter said. "Pearl just ain't made up to be Lov's woman. She don't take no interest in Lov's wants, and she don't give a cuss what nobody thinks about it. She ain't the kind of gal to be a wife to Lov. She's queer. I reckon somehow she wants to be going to Augusta, like the other gals done. None of them ever was satisfied staying here. They ain't like me, because I think more of the land than I do about staying in a durn cotton mill. You can't smell no sedge fire up there, and when it comes time to break the land for planting, you feel sick inside but you don't know what's ailing you. People has told me about that spring sickness in the mills, I don't know how many times. But when a man stays on the land, he don't get to feeling like that this time of year, because he's right here to smell the smoke of burning broom-sedge and to feel the wind fresh off the plowed fields going down inside of his body. So instead of feeling sick and not knowing what's wrong down in his body, as it happens in the durn mills, out here on the land a man feels better than he ever did. The spring-time ain't going to let you fool it by hiding away inside a durn cotton mill. It knows you got to stay on the land to feel good. That's because humans made the mills. God made the land, but you don't see Him building durn cotton mills. That's how I know better than to go up there like the rest of them. I stay where God made a place for me."

"Ellie May's acting like she was Lov's woman," Dude said.

Ada shifted the weight of her body from one foot to the other. She was standing in the same place on the porch that she had been when Lov first came into the yard. She had been watching Lov and Ellie May for a long time without looking anywhere else.

"Maybe God intended for it to be such," Jeeter said. "Maybe He knows more about it than us mortals do. God is a wise old somebody. You can't fool Him! He takes care of little details us humans never stop to think about. That's why I ain't leaving the land and going to Augusta to live in a durn cotton mill. He put me here, and He ain't never told me to get off and go up there. That's why I'm staying on the land. If I was to haul off and go to the mills, it might be hell to pay, coming and going. God might get mad because I done it and strike me dead. Or on the other hand, He might let me stay there until my natural death, but hound me all the time with little devilish things. That's the way He makes His punishment sometimes. He just lets us stay on, slow-like, and hounding us every step, until we wish we was a long time dead and in the ground. That's why I ain't going to the mills with a big rush like all them other folks around Fuller did. They got up there and all of them has a mighty pain inside for the land, but they can't come back. They got to stay now. That's what God's done to them for leaving the land. He's going to hound them every step they take until they die."

"Look at that horsing Ellie May's doing!" Dude said. "That's horsing from way back yonder!"

"By God and by Jesus, Lov," Jeeter shouted across the yard, "what about them there turnips? Has they got them damn-blasted green-gutted worms in them like mine had? I been wanting some good eating turnips since way back last spring. If Captain John hadn't sold off all his mules and shut off letting me get guano on his credit, I could have raised me a whopping big mess of turnips

23

this year. But when he sold the mules and moved to Augusta, he said he wasn't going to ruin himself by letting us tenants break him buying guano on his credit in Fuller. He said there wasn't no sense in trying to run a farm no more—fifty plows or one plow. He said he could make more money out of farming by not running plows. And that's why we ain't got no snuff and rations no more. Ada says she's just bound to have a little snuff now and then, because it sort of staves off hunger, and it does, at that. Every time I sell a load of wood I get about a dozen jars of snuff, even if I ain't got the money to buy meal and meat, because snuff is something a man is just bound to have. When I has a sharp pain in the belly, I can take a little snuff and not feel hungry all the rest of the day. Snuff is a powerful help to keep a man living.

"But I couldn't raise no turnips this year. I didn't have no mule, and I didn't have no guano. Oh, I had a few measly little rows out there in the field, but a man can't run no farm unless he's got a mule to plow it with. A hoe ain't no good except to chop cotton with, and corn. Ain't no sense in trying to grow turnips with a hoe. I reckon that's why them damn-blasted green-gutted worms got in them turnips. I didn't have no mule to cultivate them with. That's why they was all wormy.

"Have you been paying attention to what I was saying, Lov? You ain't never answered me about them turnips yet. I got a powerful gnawing in my belly for turnips. I reckon I like winter turnips just about as bad as a nigger likes watermelons. I can't see no difference between the two ways. Turnips is about the best eating I know about."

Lov did not look up. He was saying something to Ellie May, and listening to what she was saying.

Lov had always told Jeeter that he would never have anything to do with Ellie May because she had a harelip. At the time he had made a bargain with Jeeter about Pearl, he said he might consider taking Ellie May if

24

Jeeter would take her to Augusta and get a doctor to sew up her mouth. Jeeter had thought the matter over thoroughly, and decided that it would be best to let Lov take Pearl, because the cost of sewing up the harelip would probably amount to more than he was getting out of the arrangement. Letting Lov take Pearl was then all clear profit to Jeeter. Lov had given him some quilts and nearly a gallon of cylinder oil, besides giving him all of a week's pay, which was seven dollars. The money was what Jeeter wanted more than anything else, but the other things were badly needed, too.

Jeeter had been intending to take Ellie May to a doctor ever since she was three or four years old, so that when a man came to marry her there would be no drawbacks. But with first one thing and then another turning up every now and then, Jeeter had never been able to get around to it. Some day he would take her, though; he told himself that, every time he had occasion to think about it.

At the time Lov had married Pearl, he said he liked Ellie May more than he did her, but that he did not want to have a wife with a harelip. He knew the negroes would laugh at him. That was the summer before; several weeks before he had begun to like Pearl so much that he was doing everything he could think of to make her stop sleeping on a pallet on the floor. Pearl's long yellow curls hanging down her back, and her pale blue eyes, turned Lov's head. He thought there was not a more beautiful girl anywhere in the world. And for that matter, no man who had ever had the opportunity of seeing Pearl had ever gone away without thinking the same thing. It would have been impossible for her to dress herself, or even to disfigure herself, in a way that would make her plain or ordinary-looking. She became more beautiful day by day.

But Lov's wishes were unheeded. Pearl, if it was possible, was more determined than ever by that time to keep away from him. And now that Ellie May had dragged herself all the way across the yard, and was now sitting on his legs, Lov was thinking only of Ellie May. Aside from her harelip, Ellie May was just as desirable as the next girl a man would find in the sand-hill country surrounding the town of Fuller. Lov was fully aware of that. He had tried them all, white girls and black.

"Lov ain't thinking about no turnips," Dude said, in reply to his father. "Lov's wanting to hang up with Ellie May. He don't care nothing about the way her face looks now—he ain't aiming to kiss her. Ain't nobody going to kiss her, but that ain't saying nobody wouldn't fool with her. I heard niggers talking about it not long ago down the road at the old sawmill. They said she could get all the men she wanted, if she would keep her face hid."

"Quit chunking that there ball against that old house," Jeeter said angrily. "You'll have the wall worn clear in two, if you don't stop doing that all the time. The old house ain't going to stand up much longer, noway. The way you chunk that ball, it's going to pitch over and fall on the ground some of these days. I declare, I wish you had more sense than you got."

The old grandmother came hobbling out of the field with the sack of dead twigs on her back. She shuffled her feet through the deep sand of the tobacco road, and scuffed them over the hard sand of the yard, looking neither to the right nor to the left. At the bottom of the front steps she dropped the load from her shoulder and sat down to rest a while before going to the kitchen. Her groans were louder than usual, as she began rubbing her sides. Sitting on the bottom step with her feet in the sand and her chest almost touching her sharp knees, she looked more than ever like a loosely tied bag of soiled black rags. She was unmindful of the people around her, and no one was more than passingly aware that she had been any- where or had returned. If she had gone to the thicket and had not returned, no one would have known for several days that she was dead.

Jeeter watched Lov from the corners of his eyes while he tried to make another patch stick to the cracked rubber inner-tube. He had noticed that Lov was several yards from the sack of turnips, and he waited patiently while the distance grew more and more each minute. Lov had forgotten how important the safety of the turnips was. So long as Ellie May continued to tousle his hair with her hands he would forget that he had turnips. She had made him forget everything.

"What you reckon they're going to do next?" Dude said. "Maybe Lov's going to take her down to the coal chute and keep her there all day."

Ada, who had been standing on the porch all that time as motionless as one of the uprights, suddenly pulled her dress tighter over her chest. The cool February wind was barely to be felt out in the sun, but on the porch and in the shade it went straight to the bones. Ada had been ill with pellagra for several years, and she had said she was always cold except in midsummer.

"Lov's going to big her," Dude said. "He's getting ready to do it right now, too. Look at him crawl around —he acts like an old stud-horse. He ain't never let her get that close before. He said he wouldn't never get close enough to Ellie May to touch her with a stick, because he don't like the looks of her mouth. But he ain't paying no mind to it now, is he? I bet he don't even know she's got a slit-lip on her. If he does know it, he don't give a good goddam now."

Several negroes were coming up the road, walking towards Fuller. They were several hundred feet away when they first noticed the Lesters and Lov in the yard, but it was not until they were almost in front of the house that they noticed what Lov and Ellie May were doing in the farther side near a chinaberry tree. They stopped

27

laughing and talking, and slowed down until they were almost standing still.

Dude hollered at them, calling their names; but none of them spoke. They stopped and watched.

"Howdy, Captain Lov," one of them said.

Lov did not hear. The Lesters paid no more attention to the negroes. Negroes passing the house were in the habit of looking at the Lesters, but very few of them ever had anything to say. Among themselves they talked about the Lesters, and laughed about them; they spoke to other white people, stopping at their houses to talk. Lov was one of the white persons with whom they liked to talk.

Jeeter screwed the pump hose into the inner-tube valve and tried to work some air inside. The pump was rusty, the stem was bent, and the hose was cracked at the base so badly that air escaped before it ever had a chance to reach the valve. It would take Jeeter a week to pump thirty pounds of air into the tire at that rate. He could have put more air into the tires if he had attempted to blow them up with his mouth.

"It looks like I ain't going to get started to Augusta with a load of wood before next week," he said. "I wish I had a mule. I could haul a load there near about every day if I had one. The last time I drove this automobile to Augusta every one of the durn tires went flat before I could get there and back. I reckon about the best thing to do is to fill them all full of hulls and ride that way. That's what a man told me to do, and I reckon he was just about right. These old inner-tubes and tires ain't much good no longer."

The three negroes went a few steps farther down the road and stopped again. They stayed within sight of the yard, waiting to see what Lov was doing. After he had not answered them the first time they spoke, they knew he did not want them to bother him again.

Dude had thrown the baseball aside and had walked closer to Ellie May and Lov. He sat down on the ground close to them, and waited to see what they were going to do next. Lov had stopped eating turnips, and Ellie May had eaten only a part of one.

"Them niggers don't believe Lov's going to," Dude said. "They said down at the old sawmill that wouldn't nobody fool with Ellie May, unless it was in the night-time. I reckon Lov would say so himself, afterwards."

CHAPTER IV

JEETER carefully laid the pump aside and crept stealthily to the corner of the house. He propped his feet and leaned against the rotten weatherboards to wait. From where he stood, he could see everything. When Jeeter looked straight ahead, Ellie May and Lov were in full view; and if he had wanted to see Ada he could have turned his head slightly and seen her standing on the porch. There was nothing for him to do now but wait. Lov was moving farther and farther away from the sack.

Ada once more rolled the snuff stick to the other corner of her mouth. She had been watching Lov and Ellie May ever since they began getting together, and the closer they crawled to each other, the more calm she became. She was waiting, too, to ask Lov to make Pearl come to see her soon. Pearl had not been there since the day she was married.

Pearl was so much like Ada, in both appearance and behavior, that no one could have mistaken them for other than mother and daughter. When Pearl married Lov, Ada had told her she ought to run away from him before she began bearing children, and go to Augusta and live at the mills. Pearl, however, did not have the courage to run away alone. She was afraid. She did not know what would happen to her in the cotton mills, and she was too young to understand the things she heard about life there. Even though she was between twelve and thirteen years old, she was still afraid of the dark, and she often cried through most of the night as she lay trembling on her pallet on the floor. Lov was in the room, and the doors were closed, but the creep of darkness seemed to bring an unbearable feeling of strangulation. She had never told any one how much she feared the dark nights, and no one had known why she cried so much. Lov thought it was something to do with her mind. Dude did not have very much sense, and neither did one or two of the other children, and it was natural for him to think that Pearl was afflicted in the same way. The truth was, Pearl had far more sense than any of the Lesters; and that, like her hair and eyes, had been inherited from her father. The man who was her father had passed through the country one day, and had never been seen since. He had told Ada that he came from Carolina and was on his way to Texas, and that was all she knew about him.

Lately, however, Pearl was beginning to lose some of her fear. After eight months in the house with Lov she had gradually grown braver, and she had even ventured to think that some day she could run away to Augusta. She did not want to live on the sand ridge. The sight of the muddy Savannah swamps on one side and the dusty black structure of the coal chute on the other was not as beautiful as the things she had once seen in Augusta. She had been to Augusta once with Jeeter and Ada, and had seen with her own eyes girls who were laughing and care-free. She did not know whether they worked in the cotton mills, but it made little difference to her. Down there on the tobacco road no one ever laughed. Down there girls had to chop cotton in the summer, pick it in the fall, and cut fire-wood in winter.

Jeeter pushed himself erect from the corner of the house, and began moving slowly across the yard. He

31

lifted one foot, held it in the air several seconds, and put it on the ground in front of him. He had crept up on rabbits like that many times in the woods and thickets. They would be sitting in a hollow log, or in a hole in a gully, and Jeeter would creep upon them so noiselessly that they never knew how he caught them. Now he was creeping up on Lov.

Half way across the yard Jeeter suddenly broke into a terrific plunge that landed him upon the sack of turnips almost as quickly as the bat of an eye. He could have waited a few minutes longer, and reached it with the same ease with which he caught rabbits; but there was no time to lose now, and he was far more anxious to get the turnips than he had ever been to catch a rabbit.

He hugged the sack desperately in both arms, squeezing it so tight that watery turnip juice squirted through the loosely woven burlap in all directions. The juice squirted into his eyes, almost blinding him; but it was as pleasant to Jeeter as summer rain-water, and far more welcome.

Ada took one step forward, balancing herself against one of the porch uprights; Dude jumped to his feet, holding to the chinaberry tree behind him.

Lov turned around just in time to see Jeeter grab the sack and hug it in his arms. Ellie May tried to hold Lov where he was, but he succeeded in twisting out of her arms and dived for Jeeter and the turnips. Ellie May turned over just in time to clutch wildly at his foot, and he fell sprawling from mid-air to the hard ground.

Each of the Lesters, without a word having been spoken, was prepared for concerted action without delay. Dude dashed across the yard towards his father; Ada ran down the porch steps, and the old grandmother was only a few feet behind her. All of them gathered around Jeeter and the sack, waiting. Ellie May still clung to Lov's foot, pulling him back each time he succeeded in wiggling his

32

body a few inches closer to Jeeter. The tips of Lov's fingers never got closer than three feet to the sack.

"I didn't tell you no lie about Ellie May, did I?" Dude said. "Didn't I tell you right, Pa?"

"Hush up, you Dude," Ada scowled. "Can't you see your Pa ain't got no time to talk about nothing?"

Jeeter thrust his chin over the top of the sack and looked straight at Lov. Lov's eyes were bulging and blood-shot. He thought of the seven and a half miles he had walked that morning, all the way to the other side of Fuller and back again, and what he saw now made him sick.

Ellie May was doing her best to pull Lov back where he had been. He was trying to get away so he could protect his turnips and keep the Lesters out of the sack. The very thing he had at first been so careful to guard against when he stopped at the house had happened so quickly he did not know what to think about it. That, however, had been before Ellie May began sliding her bare bottom over the sandy yard towards him. He realized now what a fool he had been—to lose his head, and his turnips, too.

The three negroes were straining their necks to see everything. They had watched Ellie May and Lov with growing enthusiasm until Jeeter suddenly descended upon the sack, and now they were trying to guess what would happen next in the yard.

Ada and the old grandmother found two large and heavy sticks, and tried to pry Lov over on his back so Ellie May could reach him again. Lov was doing everything in his power to protect his sack, because he knew full well that if Jeeter once got twenty steps ahead of him, he would never be able to catch him before all the turnips were eaten. Jeeter was old, but he could run like a rabbit when he had to.

"Don't be scared of Ellie May, Lov," Ada said. "Ellie May ain't going to hurt you. She's all excited, but she ain't the rough kind at all. She won't hurt you."

33

Ada prodded him with the stick and made him stop wiggling away from Ellie May. She jabbed him in the ribs as hard as she could, biting her lower lip between her teeth.

"Them niggers look like they is going to come in the yard and help Lov out," Dude said. "If they come in here, I'll bust them with a rock. They ain't got no business helping Lov."

"They ain't thinking of coming in here," Ada said. "Niggers has got more sense than trying to interfere with white-folks' business. They don't dare come."

The colored men did not come any closer. They would have liked to help Lov, because they were friends of his, but they were more interested in waiting to see what Ellie May was going to do than they were in saving the turnips.

Ellie May was sweating like a plow-hand. Lov had got sand all over him, and she was trying to wipe it off with a corner of her gingham mother-hubbard, and to get to him again. Lov made a final and desperate plunge for the sack, and although he succeeded in getting nearly a foot closer to it, Ada hit him on the head with the blackjack stick so hard he slumped helpless on the ground with a weak groan. Ellie May was upon him in a single plunge; her excited, feline agility frightening him almost out of his mind. His breath had first been knocked from him by the force of Ellie May's weight falling on his unprotected stomach, and her knees digging into him with the pain of a mule's kick kept him from being able to breathe without sharp pains in his lungs. He was defenseless in her hold. While Ellie May held him, his arms pinned to the ground, Ada stood over him with her heavy blackjack pole, prepared to strike him on the head if he again tried to get up or to turn over on his stomach. The old grandmother waited on the other side with her stick held high and menacing above her head. She muttered under her

34

breath all the time, but no one paid any attention to what she was trying to say.

"Has these turnips got them damn-blasted green-gutted worms in them, Lov?" Jeeter said. "By God and by Jesus, if they're wormy, I don't know what I'm going to do about it. I been so sick of eating wormy turnips, I declare I almost lost my religion. It's a shame for God to let them damn-blasted green-gutted worms bore into turnips. Us poor people always gets the worse end of all deals, it looks like to me. Maybe He don't intend for humans to eat turnips at all; maybe He wants them raised for the hogs, but He don't put nothing else down here on the land in their stead. Won't nothing but turnips grow in winter-time."

Ellie May and Lov had rolled over and over a dozen or more times, like tumble-bugs; when they finally stopped, Lov was on top. Ada had followed them across the yard, and the grandmother too, and they stood ready to club Lov with the blackjack poles if he showed the first sign of trying to get up before Ellie May was ready to release him.

While the others were in the far corner of the yard, Jeeter suddenly jumped to his feet, hugging the sack of turnips tight to his stomach, and ran out across the tobacco road towards the woods beyond the old cotton field. He did not pause to look back over his shoulder until he was nearly half a mile away. In another moment he had disappeared into the woods.

The negroes were laughing so hard they could not stand up straight. They were not laughing at Lov, it was the actions of the Lesters that appeared so funny to them. Ada's serious face and Ellie May's frantic determination furnished a scene none of them could look at without laughing. They waited until every one had quieted down, and then they went slowly down the road towards Fuller talking about what they had seen in the Lester yard.

35

Ada and the grandmother presently went back to the porch and sat down on the steps to watch Ellie May and Lov. There was no longer any danger of him getting away. He did not even try to get up now.

"How many scoops-full does that No. 17 freight engine empty at the chute every morning, Lov?" Dude said. "Looks like to me them freight engines take on nearly twice as much coal as the passenger ones do. Them firemen on the freights is always chunking big hunks of coal at the nigger cabins along the track. I reckon that's why they have to take on more coal than the passengers do. The passenger trains go faster, and the nigger firemen don't have a chance to chunk out coal at the nigger cabins. I've seen near about a whole scoop-full of coal chunked out of the freights at one time. The railroad don't know nothing about it, do they? If they did, they'd make the fireman stop that. They throw out more coal along the tracks than the engines burn, near about, I bet. That's why niggers don't have to cut wood all the time. They all burn railroad coal in their cabins."

Lov was too breathless to say anything.

"Why don't you burn coal in your house, instead of wood, Lov? Nobody would know about it. I ain't going to tell on you, if you want to do that. It's a lot easier than cutting wood every day."

Mother Lester, the old grandmother, sitting beside her bag of dead twigs, began groaning again and rubbing her sides with her fists. Presently she got up, lifted the bag over her shoulder, and went into the house towards the kitchen. She made a fire in the cook-stove and sat down beside it to wait until the twigs burned out. She was certain Jeeter would not bring any of the turnips back for her to eat. He would stay in the thicket and eat every one of them himself. While she waited for the fire to die down, she looked into the snuff jar on the shelf, but it was still empty. There had been no snuff in it for nearly a week,

36

and Ada would not tell her where the full jar was hidden. The only time she ever had any snuff was when she accidently found the jar hidden away somewhere, and took some before anybody could stop her. Jeeter had knocked her down several times about doing that, and he had said he would kill her if he ever caught her stealing snuff again. There were times when she would have been willing to die, if she could only have for once all the snuff she wanted.

"Why don't the firemen blow the whistles more than they do, Lov?" Dude said. "They hardly blow the whistles at all. If I was a fireman I'd pull the whistle cord near about all the time. They make a noise about as pretty as an automobile horn does."

Dude sat on the pine stump until Lov got up and staggered across the yard towards the tobacco road. Lov looked all around in every direction, hoping he might see Jeeter hiding somewhere close. He was sure that Jeeter had gone to the pine woods beyond the old cotton field though, and he knew it would be a waste of time trying to find him and catch him. It was too late to stop him now.

Ellie May lay where she was; stretched out flat on the ground, on her back. Perspiration had matted her hair against her forehead and neck, and her pink gingham dress was twisted under her shoulders and head in such a way that it made a pillow for her to lie on. Her mouth looked as if it had been torn; her flaming red upper gum looked like a bleeding, painful wound under her left nostril. Her divided lip quivered, and her body trembled.

"You ought to give me them overalls when you're done with them," Dude said. "I ain't had a new pair of overalls since I can remember. Pa says he's going to buy me and him both some one of these days when he sells a lot of wood, but I ain't putting none too much trust in what he says. He ain't going to sell no wood, not more than a load at a time, noway. He tells more lies than any man I ever heard of. I reckon he'd rather lie about it than haul wood to Augusta. He's that lazy he won't get up off the ground sometimes when he stumbles. I've seen him stay there near about an hour before he got up. He's the laziest son of a bitch I ever seen."

Lov went to the middle of the road and stood there uncertainly, his legs wide apart to keep his balance, and his body swaying backward and forward like a drunken man's. He began brushing the sand off of his clothes, and shaking it out of his hair. Sand was in his pockets and shoes, and even his ears were full of it.

"When is you going to buy yourself an automobile, Lov?" Dude asked. "You make a heap of a lot of money at the chute—you ought to buy yourself a great big car, like the ones the rich people in Augusta has got. I'll show you how to run it. I know all about automobiles. Pa's old Ford ain't much to look at now, but when it was in good running order I used to run the wheels off of it sometimes, near about. You ought to get one that has got a great big horn on it. Whistles and horns make a pretty sound, don't they, Lov? When is you going to get you an automobile?"

Lov stood in the middle of the road for the next ten or fifteen minutes, looking out over the top of the sagging brown broom-sedge towards the thicket where Jeeter was. After he had waited until he did not know what else to do, he staggered up the road in the direction of his house and the coal chute. Pearl would be at the house when he reached it, but as soon as he walked inside she would run out the back door and stay until he left. Even if she did not leave the room when he entered the house, she would not look at him nor have anything to say. He could look at her long yellow hair hanging down her back, but that was all. She would not allow him to come close enough to look into her eyes; if he tried to do that, she would certainly run off into the broom-sedge.

Ada and Dude watched him until he was out of sight

38

beyond the rise in the ridge, and then they turned their backs and looked at Ellie May in the yard.

Dude went to the pine stump and sat down to watch the red wood-ants crawl over the stomach and breasts of his sister. The muscles of her legs and back twitched nervously for a while, and then slowly the jerking stopped altogether, and she lay still. Her mouth was partly open, and her upper lip looked as if it had been torn wider apart than it naturally was. The perspiration had dried on her forehead and cheeks, and smudges of dirt were streaked over her pale white skin.

For nearly an hour she slept deeply in the warm February sun, and when she awoke, her right arm was lying across her mouth where Dude had placed it when he left the yard to get some of the turnips before his father had eaten them all.

CHAPTER V

DOWN in the thicket, hidden from the house and road by the four-foot wall of brown broom-sedge, Jeeter's conscience began to bother him. His hunger had been abated temporarily, and his overalls pockets were filled with turnips, but the slowly formed realization that he had stolen his son-in-law's food sickened his body and soul. He had stolen food before, food and everything else he had had opportunity to take, but each time, as now, he regretted what he had done until he could convince himself that he had not done anything so terribly wrong. Sometimes he could do this in a few minutes, at other times it was days, and even weeks, before he was satisfied that God had forgiven him and would not punish him too much.

The sound of Dude's voice behind him in the woods was like the voice of God calling him to punishment. Dude had been crashing through the thicket and beating the underbrush with a blackjack stick for the past half hour trying to find Jeeter before all the turnips had been eaten.

There was a hollow silence in the woods around Jeeter between Dude's yells, and Jeeter felt humble and penitent. He carefully wiped the blade of the knife with which he had pared the turnips, and thrust it into his pocket. Then he jumped up and ran out of the thicket and into the broom-sedge. He could see the roof of the house and the tops of the chinaberry trees, but he had no way of knowing whether Lov had gone home.

Dude saw him the moment he came out of the under-brush and started through the sedge.

"Hey! Where you running off to now?" Dude shouted at him, running across the field to cut Jeeter off from the house.

Jeeter stopped and waited for Dude to reach him. He took out half a dozen of the smallest turnips and laid them in Dude's outstretched hands.

"What made you run off and try to eat them all up for, and not give me none?" Dude demanded. "You ain't the only one what likes turnips. I ain't had no more to eat this week than you has. You're as mean as an old snake at times. Why didn't you want me to have none?"

"The good Lord is against theft," Jeeter said. "He don't make no provision for the future for them that steals. They has got to look out for theirselves in the after-life. Now I got to get right with God and confess my sins. I done an evil deed this day. God don't like for His people to do that. He won't take no notice of sinners. And theft is the worse deed a human can do, near about."

"Hell," Dude said, "you talk like that near about every time you steal something, but you don't never stick to it afterwards. You're just trying to keep from giving me some more turnips. You can't fool me."

"That's a sinful thing to say about a man who's tried all his life to stand right with God. God's on my side, and He don't like to hear people talking about me in that manner. You ought not to talk like that, Dude. Ain't you got no sense at all?"

"Give me some more," Dude said. "Ain't no use for you to try to keep them all by talking like that. That ain't going to get you nowhere. That don't mean nothing to me. I know better than to get fooled this time."

41

"You've already had five, ain't you?" Jeeter said, counting the ones he had left in his pockets. "You don't need no more."

Dude thrust his hand into the nearest pocket and jerked out as many as he could hold in his hand. Jeeter hit at him with his elbows, but Dude did not mind that. Jeeter was too weak to hurt him.

"That's all you're going to have," Jeeter said. "I'm taking what's left and give to Ada and Ellie May. I expect they be almost as hungry as I was. They'll be waiting now to get some. Has Lov gone yet?"

"He went back to the chute long ago," Dude said.

They started walking through the broom-sedge towards the house. Long before they reached the road they could see Ada and Ellie May waiting in the yard for them. The grandmother was crouching in the doorway, afraid to come out any farther.

"I reckon the women folks is pretty hungry, too," Dude said. "Ellie May's belly was growling all last night. It woke me up this morning, starting all over again."

Ellie May and Ada sat down on the steps when Dude and Jeeter came into view. They waited patiently while Dude and Jeeter broke through the broom-sedge, and as they came nearer, Ada went up on another step. The grandmother crouched in the doorway, clinging to the frame with both hands. None of them was more hungry than she was.

There was another woman in the porch, too. She sat swaying backward and forward in the rocking-chair, and singing a hymn at the top of her voice. Each time she reached the highest note she could go, she held it until her breath gave out and then she started all over again.

Jeeter jumped over the drain ditch and came across the yard with Dude at his heels. As soon as he saw the woman in the rocking-chair his face brightened, and he almost stumbled in his haste to reach her.

"The good Lord be praised!" he shouted, seeing Bessie
Rice sitting on the porch. "I knowed God would send
His angel to take away my sins. Sister Bessie, the Lord
knows what I needed, all right. He wants me to give up
my sinful ways, don't He?"

Ada and Ellie May jerked at Jeeter's overalls' pockets,
extracting the remaining turnips in desperate hurry.
Jeeter tossed three of the smallest ones on the porch in the
direction of the door. The grandmother fell on her knees
and clutched them hungrily against her stomach, while
she munched the vegetable with her toothless gums.

"The Lord told me to come to the Lester house," the
woman preacher said. "I was at home sweeping out the
kitchen when He came to me and said, 'Sister Bessie,
Jeeter Lester is doing something evil. You go to his place
and pray for him right now before it's too late, and try to
make him give up his evil goings-on.' I looked right back
at the Lord, and said, 'Lord, Jeeter Lester is a powerful
sinful man, but I'll pray for him until the devil goes clear
back to hell.' That's what I told Him, and here I is. I
came to pray for you and yours, Jeeter Lester. Maybe it
ain't too late yet to get on the good side of the Lord. It's
people like you who ought to be good, instead of letting
the devil make you do all sorts of sinful things."

"I knowed the good Lord wouldn't let me slip and fall
in the devil's hands!" Jeeter shouted, dancing around
Bessie's chair. "I knowed it! I knowed it! I always been
on God's side, even when things was the blackest, and I
knowed He'd jerk me out of hell before it was too late. I
ain't no sinner by nature, Sister Bessie. It's just the old
devil who's always hounding me to do a little something
bad. But I ain't going to do it. I want to go to heaven
when I die."

"Ain't you going to give me a turnip, Jeeter?" she said.
"I ain't had so much to eat lately. Times is hard for the
good and bad alike, though I sometimes think that's not

43

just exactly right. The good ought never be hard put to it, like the sinful ought to be all the time."

"Sure, Bessie," Jeeter said, giving her several turnips. He selected the largest ones he could find. "I know how you like to eat, about as bad as the rest of us. I wish I had something to give you to take home. When I had plenty, I used to give Brother Rice a whole armful of chickens and sweet potatoes at a time. Now I ain't got nothing but a handful of measly little turnips, but I ain't ashamed of them. The Lord growed them. His doings is good enough for me. Ain't they for you?"

Sister Bessie smiled happily at Jeeter and his family. She was always happy when she could pray for a sinner and save him from the devil, because she had been a sinner herself before Brother Rice chased the devil out of her and married her. Her husband was dead now though, and she was carrying on his work in the sand hills. He had left her eight hundred dollars in insurance money when he died the summer before, and she was saving it to carry on his work when the time came that it was needed most. She had the money in a bank in Augusta.

Some of the people in the sand hills said the kind of religion Sister Bessie talked about was far from being God's idea of what consecrated people should say and do. Every time she heard it, Bessie always said that the other people did not know any more about God's religion than the male preachers who talked about it knew. Most of them belonged to no sect at all, while the rest were Hard-shell Baptists. Bessie hated Hard-shell Baptists with the same intensity with which she hated the devil.

There was no church building to house Bessie's congregation, nor was there an organized band of communicants to support her. She went from house to house in the sand hills, mostly along the crest of the ridge where the old tobacco road was, and prayed for people who needed prayer and wanted it. She was past thirty-five, almost

44

forty, and she was much better-looking than most women in the sand hills, except for her nose.

Bessie's nose had failed to develop properly. There was no bone in it, and there was no top to it. The nostrils were exposed, and Dude had once said that when he looked at her nose it was like looking down the end of a double-barrel shotgun. Bessie was sensitive about the appearance of it, and she tried to keep people from staring at her and commenting on what they saw.

Ada had already told Bessie about the turnips Jeeter took from Lov. Bessie had come prepared to pray for Jeeter for his sins in general, but she was glad she had a specific sin to pray for him to God about. Prayer always did a man more good, she said, if there was something he was ashamed of.

First of all though, she finished eating all the turnips Jeeter would let her have.

"I wish Lov was here so I could ask his forgiveness," Jeeter said. "I reckon I'll have to go down to his house the first thing in the morning and tell him how powerful sorry I am. I hope he ain't so mad about it that he'll try to beat me with a stick. He's got a whopping big temper when he gets good and mad about something."

"Let's have a little prayer," Bessie said, swallowing the last of the turnip.

"The good Lord be praised," Jeeter said. "I'm sure glad you came when you did, Sister Bessie, because I'm needing prayer about as bad as I ever did. I was a sinful man to-day. The Lord don't take up with humans who commits theft. I don't know what made me so bad. I reckon the old devil just came along and got the upper hand on me."

Every one got down on his knees, except Ellie May and Dude. They sat on the steps eating and watching.

"You know," Bessie said, "some people make an objection to kneeling down and having prayer out of doors.

45

They don't like to have me pray for them on the front porch or in the yard. They say, 'Sister Bessie, can't we go in the house out of sight and pray there just as good?' And do you know what I tell them? I say, 'Brothers and Sisters, I ain't ashamed to pray out here in the open. I want folks passing along the road to know I'm on God's side. I ain't ashamed to let folks see me pray. It's the old devil that's always whispering about going in the house out of sight.' That's the way I stick up for the Lord. I kneel right down and pray in the big road just as loud as I do in a schoolhouse or at a camp-meeting. I ain't ashamed to pray in the front yard or on the porch. It's the old devil who's always telling folks to go in the house out of sight."

"The good Lord be praised," Jeeter said.

"Let's get ready to pray," she said.

Ada and Jeeter bowed their heads and closed their eyes. Mother Lester knelt in the doorway, but she did not close her eyes. She stared straight ahead of her, out over the field of brown broom-sedge.

"Dear God, here I is again to offer a little prayer for sinful people. Jeeter Lester and his family want me to pray for them again. The last time helped them a whole lot, and if it wasn't for Jeeter getting in the clutch of the devil to-day, there wouldn't be no need for prayer this soon again. But Jeeter let the devil get hold of him, and he went and done a powerful sinful thing. He stole all of Lov's turnips and wouldn't give them back. They're all et up now, so it's too late to take them to Lov. That's why we want to pray for Jeeter. You ought to make him stop stealing like he does. I never seen a more stealing man in all my days. It looks like he takes to stealing just as naturally as one of us takes a drink of water. But Jeeter wants to quit, though it seems like he goes and does it again almost as soon as we get through praying for him. You ought to make him quit it this time for good and all. Ain't no sense in You letting a man just keep on doing a sinful

46

thing all the time. You ought to put a stop to it and not let him do it no more. You ain't going to let the old devil tell You what to do, is You? That ain't no way for the Lord to do. The Lord ought to tell the devil to get away and stop trying to tempt good folks.

"And Sister Ada has got the pleurisy again pretty bad. You ought to do something for her this time, sure enough. The last time didn't help her none too much. She can't do all her household work when she's got the pleurisy so bad. If You'll make her well of it, she'll quit the devil for all time. Won't you, Sister Ada?"

"Yes, Lord!"

"And old Mother Lester has got a misery in her sides. She's in pain all the time with it. She's kneeling down right now, but she is in such pain she can't do it many more times.

"You ought to bless Ellie May, too. Ellie May has got that slit in her lip that makes her an awful sight to look at. If You was to make ———"

"Don't forget to pray for Pearl, Sister Bessie," Jeeter said. "Pearl needs praying for something awful."

"What has Pearl done sinful, Brother Jeeter?"

"Well, that was what Lov wanted to speak to me about to-day. He says Pearl won't talk to him, and she won't let him touch her. When night comes, she gets down and sleeps on a durn pallet on the floor. Lov has got to sleep in the bed by himself, and can't get her to take no interest in him. That's a pretty bad thing for a wife to do, and God ought to make her quit it. Lov is due some rights. A woman ain't got no business sleeping on a durn pallet on the floor, noway."

"Maybe she knows best, Brother Jeeter," Bessie said. "Maybe Pearl is going to have a little baby, and that's her way of telling Brother Lov about it."

"No, it ain't that, Sister Bessie. Lov says he ain't never slept with her yet. He says he ain't never touched her yet,

47

neither. That's what's worrying him so durn much. He wants her to sleep in the bed with him and stop getting down on that durn pallet on the floor every night like she does. Pearl needs praying for to make her quit that sleeping down there on the floor."

"Brother Jeeter, little girls like Pearl don't know how to live married lives like we grown-up women do. So maybe if I was to talk to her myself instead of getting God to do it, she would change her ways. I expect I know more about what to tell her than He does, because I been a married woman up to the past summer when my former husband died. I expect I know all about it. God wouldn't know what to tell her."

"That might help some, but if I was the praying kind myself, I reckon I'd sort of tell God about it and maybe He would do some good. Maybe He's run across gals like that before, though I don't believe there's another durn gal in the whole country who's as contrary-minded about sleeping in the bed as Pearl is."

Dude picked up the baseball and began tossing it on the roof of the porch, and catching it when it rolled down into the yard. The ball knocked loose the rotten shingles, and pieces of them showered the yard. Ellie May sat waiting to hear some more prayer when Bessie and Jeeter got through talking about Pearl.

"Maybe it wouldn't hurt none if I was to mention it," Bessie said.

"That's right," Jeeter said. "You speak to the Lord about it, too. Both of you together ought to get something done about it."

"Now, Lord, I've got something special to pray about. I don't ask favors unless they is things I want pretty bad, so this time I'm asking for a favor for Pearl. I want You to make her stop sleeping on a pallet on the floor while Brother Lov has to sleep by himself in the bed. Make Pearl get in the bed, Lord, and make her stay there where she belongs. She ain't got no right to sleep on a pallet on the floor when Lov's got a bed for her. Now, You make her stop acting like she's been, and put her in the bed when night comes. I was a good wife to my former husband. I never slept on no pallet on the floor. Sister Ada here don't do nothing like that. And when I marry another man, I ain't going to do that, neither. I'm going to get in the bed just as big as my new husband does. So You tell Pearl to quit that. We women knows what we ought to do, and Pearl just ain't old enough to know better. You got to tell her to quit doing that. If it was ———"

"What was that you was saying about getting married, Sister Bessie?" Jeeter asked. "Didn't I hear you say you was going to marry yourself a new husband? Who is you going to get married to?"

"Well, I ain't made up my mind yet. I been looking around some, though. Right now it looks like I can't make up my mind. It's my wish to find a man who's got some goods and possessions, but it looks like ain't nobody got nothing around here no more. All the men folks is poor."

"Now, if it wasn't for Ada, there," Jeeter said.

"Brother Jeeter, you hush your mouth!" she giggled. "You make me feel so funny when you talk like that! How'd you know I'd take to you? You're pretty old, ain't you?"

"I reckon you'd better finish up the prayer," he said. "Ada, there, gets sort of peeved when I talk about marrying another woman."

"—Save us from the devil and make a place for us in heaven. Amen."

CHAPTER VI

"You clear forgot to say a little prayer for Dude," Jeeter said suddenly. "You left Dude out all around, Bessie. Dude, he's as big a sinner as the rest of us Lesters."

Bessie jumped up and ran out into the yard. She clutched Dude by the arm and dragged him to the porch by her chair. She kneeled down in front of it, and tried to pull Dude down beside her.

"I don't want to do that," Dude said angrily. "I don't want no praying for me. I ain't done nothing. Pa did all the stealing of Lov's turnips. He took them and ran off to the thicket."

Bessie took his hands in hers and stroked his arms for several minutes without speaking. Then she stood up beside him and locked her arms around his waist. She squeezed him so hard it made the blood rush to his head.

"I got to pray for you, Dude. The Lord told me all you Lesters was sinful. He didn't leave you out no more than He did Ellie May."

Dude looked into her face. She pleaded convincingly enough to make him want to be prayed for, but he could not stop looking down into her nostrils.

"What you laughing at, Dude?" she said.

"Nothing," he snickered, twisting his head until he could almost see behind himself.

"There ain't nothing about prayer to laugh at, Dude,"

she said. "All of us has got to have it some time or another."

He felt ill at ease standing so close to her. The way she stroked his arms and shoulders with her hands made him nervous, and he could not stand still.

"Quit that jumping up and down, Dude," Jeeter said. "What ails you?"

Bessie drew her arms tighter around his waist, and smiled at him.

"You kneel down beside me and let me pray for you. You'll do that, won't you, Dude?"

He put his arms around her neck, and began rubbing her as she was rubbing him.

"Hell," he said, snickering again, "I don't give a damn if I do."

"I knowed you would want me to pray for you, Dude," she said. "It will help you get shed of your sins, like Jeeter did."

They knelt down on the porch floor beside the chair. Dude continued to rub her shoulders, and Bessie kept her arms around him. Jeeter was sitting on the floor behind them, leaning against the wall of the house and waiting to hear the prayer for Dude.

"Dear God, I'm asking You to save Brother Dude from the devil and make a place for him in heaven. That's all. Amen."

Bessie stopped praying, but neither she nor Dude made an effort to stand up.

"Praise the Lord," Jeeter said, "but that was a durn short prayer for a sinner like Dude."

"Dude don't need no more praying for. He's just a boy, and he's not sinful like us grown-ups is. He ain't sinful like you is, Jeeter."

"Well, maybe you is right," Jeeter said, "but Dude, he cusses all the time at me and his Ma. He ain't got no respect for none of us. Maybe that's as it should be, but I

51

sort of recollect the Bible saying a son shouldn't cuss his Ma and Pa like he does other people. Nobody never told me no different, but somehow it don't seem right for him to do that. I've seen him pestering Ellie May with a stick, too, and I know that ain't right. That's sinful, and it ought to be prayed about."

"Dude won't do that again," Bessie said, stroking Dude's hair. "He's a fine boy, Dude is. He would make a handsome preacher, too. He's mighty like my former husband in his younger days. I sort of feel like there ain't much difference between them now."

Ada twisted around to see why Dude was staying on the porch. He and Bessie were still kneeling down beside the chair, with their arms around each other.

"Dude's sixteen years old now," Jeeter said. "That makes him two years younger than Ellie May. Well, pretty soon he'll be getting a wife, I reckon. All my other male children married early in life, just like the gals done. When Dude gets married, I won't have none of my children left with me, except Ellie May. And I don't reckon she'll ever find a man to marry her. It's all on account of that mouth she's got. I been thinking I'd take her up to Augusta and get a doctor to sew up her lip. She'd marry quick enough then, because she's got a powerful way with her, woman-like. Ain't nothing wrong with her, excepting that slit in her lip. If it wasn't for that, she'd been married as quick as Pearl was. Men here around Fuller all want to marry gals about eleven or twelve years old, like Pearl was. Ada, there, was just turning twelve when I married her."

"The Lord intended all of us should be mated," Bessie said. "He made us that way. That's what my former husband used to say. I'd tell him that a man needs a woman, and he'd say a woman needs a man. My former husband was just like the Lord in that respect. They both believed in the same thing when it came to mating."

"I reckon the Lord did intend for all of us to get mated," Jeeter said, "but He didn't take into account a woman with a slit in her mouth like Ellie May's got. I don't believe He done the right thing by her when He opened up her lip like that. That's the only contrary thing I ever said about the Lord, but it's the truth. What use is a slit like that for? You can't spit through it, and you can't whistle through it, now can you? It was just meanness on His part when He done that. That's what it was—durn meanness."

"You shouldn't talk about the Lord like that. He knows what He done it for. He knows everything. He wouldn't have done it if He didn't have a good purpose in mind. He knows what He makes men and women for. He made Ellie May's face like that with a good reason in mind. He had the best reason in the world for doing it."

"What reason?"

"Maybe I ought not to say it, Jeeter."

"It ain't no secret between you and the Lord, is it, Sister Bessie?"

"No, ain't no secrets between us. But I know."

"You know what?"

"Why He made her lip slit open."

"Ain't you going to tell me?"

"Brother Jeeter, He done that to her lip to save her pure body from the wicked men."

"What men? I'm the only man around here."

"It's you, Brother Jeeter."

"I ain't wicked. I'm sinful at rare times, but I never been wicked."

"It's all the same to God. It don't make no difference to Him which it is."

"What did I do? I don't see how stealing a few measly turnips and sweet potatoes once in a while has anything to do with Ellie May's face."

"Brother Jeeter, the Lord done that to her lip to save

53

her pure body from being ruined by you. He knowed she would be safe in this house when He made her like that. He knowed that you was once a powerful sinner, and that you might be again if———"

"That's the truth," Jeeter said. "I used to be a powerful sinful man in my time. I reckon I was at one time the most powerful sinful man in the whole country. Now, you take them Peabody children over across the field. I reckon clear near about all of them is half mine, one way or another. And then I used to———"

"You wait till I finish accusing you, Jeeter, before you start lying out of it."

"I ain't lying out of it, Bessie. I just now told you how powerful sinful I once was. There was a man and his wife moved here from———"

"As I was saying, you didn't keep none of it hid from the Lord———"

"But Henry Peabody didn't know nothing about it though———"

"—He knowed that you might take it into your head to ruin Ellie May. The Lord knows everything, and He's got his reasons. He knowed you was such a powerful sinful man long years ago that you wouldn't have obeyed Him if He told you to take your eyes out, if your eyes offended Him."

"Looking at her slit with my eyes won't offend nobody. He don't care about my eyes. What would He want to take them out for?"

"Just like I was saying. If the Lord had told you to cut your eyes out because they offended Him, you wouldn't have done it. That showed you was a powerful sinner. Or if He had told you to cut off your hand, or your ears, for the same reason, you wouldn't have obeyed Him. And He knowed if He told you to stop fooling with Ellie May, you wouldn't have cut off the root of the evil like He said do. That's the reason He sent Ellie May into the world

54

with a slit in her lip. He figured she would be safe from a sinner like you, because you wouldn't like the looks of her."

"The Lord be praised," Jeeter said. "You sure have opened my eyes to the way of God. I never knowed before about that, I declare. If I had knowed it, I sure would have cut myself off when I was fooling around over there at Peabody's. Then if I had done that, Ellie May wouldn't look like she does now, would she, Bessie?"

"It's just like I said. The Lord knows more about us humans' ways than we do."

"I've been a powerful sinful man in my time, I reckon. I never knowed I ought to cut myself off before. Maybe it's not too late now. I sure don't want to let the devil get hold of me."

Bessie turned to Dude again, smiling at him and holding her arms tighter around his neck. Dude did not know what to do next. He liked to touch her, and feel her, and he wanted her to hug him some more, as she had done. He liked to feel her arms tight around him, and have her rub him. Yet he could not believe that Bessie was hugging him for any real reason. She had stopped praying fifteen minutes before, but she still made no motion to release him and make him get up.

"Say, Sister Bessie," Jeeter said, leaning forward and squinting his eyes under his heavy black brows, "what in hell is you and Dude doing there? You and him has been squatting there, hugging and rubbing of the other, for near about half an hour."

Dude hoped she would not make him get up, because he liked to feel her pull him tight to her breast and squeeze him in her arms.

Bessie tried to stand up, but Dude would not let her. She sat down again beside him on the floor, running her fingers through his hair.

"Durn if I ever saw a woman preacher take on like

55

that before," Jeeter said, shaking his head. "Looks to me like you ain't going to do no more praying to-day. You and Dude is hugging and rubbing of the other, ain't you? By God and by Jesus, if it ain't so!"

Bessie got up and sat down in the chair. She tried to make Dude go away, but he stood in front of her, waiting for her to touch him.

"The Lord was speaking to me," she said. "He was telling me I ought to marry a new husband. I can't get around much by myself, and if I was to get married to a man, maybe I could do more preaching and praying. The Lord would turn him into a preacher too, and both of us could travel around spreading the gospel."

"He didn't tell you to marry Dude, did He? Dude ain't no preacher. He ain't got sense enough to be one. He wouldn't know what to preach about when the time came to get up and say something."

"Dude would make a fine preacher," she interrupted. "Dude would be just about as good at preaching and praying as my former husband was, maybe better. The Lord and me could show him how to do. It ain't hard at all after you catch on to it."

"I wish I was in my younger days. If I was, I could maybe do it myself with you. I could do it yet, only Ada, there, has got so she don't want me fooling with the women-folks no more. I know I could do as fine preaching and praying as the next one. It ain't that what's holding me back—it's Ada, there. She's got a queer notion that I might take to fooling with the women-folks. Well, I ain't saying I wouldn't if I had half a chance, neither."

"It would require a younger man for me to be satisfied," Bessie said. "Dude there is just suitable for preaching and living with me. Ain't you, Dude?"

"You want me to go home with you now?" he said.

"I got to pray over it first, Dude," she said. "When I come back by here the next time, I'll let you know. You'll

56

have to wait until I can ask the Lord if you'll do. He's sometimes particular about his male preachers, especially if they is going to marry women preachers."

Bessie ran down the steps and over the hard white sand of the yard. When she reached the tobacco road, she turned around and looked at the Lesters on the front porch several minutes.

Presently, without waiting to walk, she began running through the deep white sand towards her house two miles away on the bluff above the Savannah.

Bessie's home, a tenant house of three rooms, and a corn-crib, sat on the edge of the bluff. That was where the country dropped down into the swampy Savannah River Valley. The house, covered with unpainted weatherboards, sat precariously on three piles of thin stones. The fourth pile had fallen down ten or twelve years before, making one end of the house sag to the ground.

"Well," Jeeter said, "Sister Bessie is up to something, all right. It looks to me like she's got her head set on marrying Dude, there. I never seen such hugging and rubbing of the other as them two was doing. Something is going to come of it. Something is bound to happen."

Dude snickered and stood behind a chinaberry tree so nobody could see him. Ellie May watched him from behind the pine stump, smiling because she had heard what Bessie had said.

Jeeter sat looking out over the old field of brown broom-sedge, and wondering if he could borrow a mule somewhere and raise a crop that year. The time for spring plowing had already arrived, and it made him restless. He did not like to sit idly on the porch and let the spring pass, without burning and plowing. He had decided that he could at least burn over the fields, even if he did not yet know how he could get a mule and seed-cotton and guano. He would have gone out then and set the broom-sedge on fire; but he felt comfortable where he

57

was, and the burning of the fields could wait until the next day. There was plenty of time left yet. It would not take him long to put in a crop when once he got started.

Now that he was alone he began to worry all over again about the way he had treated Lov. He wanted to do something to make amends. If he went down to the chute the next morning and told Lov how sorry he was and that he promised never to steal anything from him again, he hoped that Lov would forgive him and not try to hit him with chunks of coal. And while he was about it, he could stop by Lov's house and speak to Pearl. He would tell her that she had to stop sleeping on a pallet on the floor, and be more considerate of Lov's wants. It was bad enough, he knew, to have to put up with a woman all day long, and then when night came to be left alone, was even worse.

"Ain't you going to haul no more wood to Augusta?" Ada demanded. "I ain't had no new snuff since I don't know when. And all the meal is gone, and the meat, too. Ain't nothing in the house to eat."

"I'm aiming to take a load over there to-morrow or the next day," Jeeter said. "Don't hurry me, woman. It takes a heap of time to get ready to make a trip over there. I got my own interests to consider. You keep out of it."

"You're just lazy, that's what's wrong with you. If you wasn't lazy you could haul a load every day, and I'd have me some snuff when I wanted it most."

"I got to be thinking about farming the land," Jeeter said. "I ain't no durn woodchopper. I'm a farmer. Them woodchoppers hauling wood to Augusta ain't got no farming to take up their time, like I has. Why, I expect I'm going to grow near about fifty bales of cotton this year, if I can borrow the mules and get some seed-cotton and guano on credit in Fuller. By God and by Jesus, I'm a farmer. I ain't no durn woodchopper."

"That's the way you talk every year about this time,

58

but you don't never get started. It's been seven or eight years since you turned a furrow. I been listening to you talk about taking up farming again so long I don't believe nothing you say now. It's a big old whopping lie. All you men is like that. There's a hundred more just like you all around here, too. None of you is going to do nothing, except talk. The rest of them go around begging, but you're so lazy you won't even do that."

"Now, Ada," Jeeter said, "I'm going to start in the morning. Soon as I get all the fields burned off, I'll go borrow me some mules. Me and Dude can grow a bale to the acre, if I can get me some seed-cotton and guano."

"Humph!" Ada said, leaving the porch.

CHAPTER VII

JEETER did not go down to the coal chute to see Lov. Neither did he go to the house to speak to Pearl.

There were always well-developed plans in Jeeter's mind for the things he intended doing; but somehow he never got around to doing them. One day led to the next, and it was much more easy to say he would wait until tomorrow. When that day arrived, he invariably postponed action until a more convenient time. Things had been going along in that easy way for almost a lifetime now; nevertheless, he was again getting ready to burn off the fields and plow the land. He wanted to raise a crop of cotton.

Having an operation performed on Ellie May's lip was one of those things that Jeeter had been waiting for fifteen years to do. Several times each year he had said he was going to take her to a doctor in Augusta; when he did make an effort to take her there, he usually never got any farther than the store at the crossroad, where something was certain to come up that caused him to change his plans.

In the course of all those years he had actually reached Augusta two or three times with the sole intention of having the operation performed; but it had always resulted in something coming to his mind at the last minute that he thought he needed more than Ellie May needed an operation. Once it was plow-lines that he could not do without another day, even though he had no mule to use them on; another time it was snuff he had to have, and so he had stopped at the store and spent what little money he had, and they returned home with nothing accomplished.

Ellie May did not protest. She could not have been made to believe that her harelip could be sewn together in such a way that only the faintest suggestion of a scar would remain. She had become so accustomed to the gaping narrow opening in her mouth that she could not believe that it was possible for her ever to look any different from the way she always had.

On those very few occasions when Jeeter had made preparations to go to the hospital, and when he had talked to Ellie May about going there, she would stand behind the corner of the house, or behind one of the many chinaberry trees scattered around the house, and grin. The Lesters had spoken so frequently about her harelip that she had come to believe that Jeeter's proposal to have it operated upon was merely another way of making fun of her appearance. She remained hidden behind the house or a chinaberry tree until the subject of conversation was changed, and only came out where she could be seen when she was certain nothing more would be said about her.

"It ain't no sin to look like that, Ellie May," Jeeter had told her. "You came into the world that way from God, and that's the way He intended for you to look. Sometimes I think maybe it would be a sin to change it, because that would be doing over something He made."

"Well, all I got to say," Ada had stated, "is that it's a shame He didn't make Dude with the slit instead of Ellie May. A gal ain't got no business looking like that. Women ain't good for nothing but to marry and work for men, and when one of them has that kind of thing on her, there

61

ain't no man I ever heard of who's going to use her. If it was Dude who had the slit, it wouldn't make no difference at all. Men ain't noticed so much in the face as women is, noway."

Once when Ellie May went to the schoolhouse several years before, to enter the first grade, she returned home before noon and never went back again. The teacher told her she was too old to attend school with little children, but the real reason for sending her home was because the other boys and girls laughed at her harelip so much they could not study their lessons. So Ellie May came back home and never went again. Dude had never attended school, either; Jeeter said he was needed at home to help him do the work.

But if Jeeter was indifferent towards Ellie May's need for an operation, there was one thing in his life he tried to do with all the strength in his mind and body. That one thing was the farming of the land. There had been scarcely a moment in his life during the past six or seven years when he was not thinking about it, and trying to discover some way by which he could raise cotton. When Captain John had moved to Augusta seven years before, it seemed to be the end of all farming as far as Jeeter was concerned, but he would not give up the struggle to break the land each spring and plant cotton.

Jeeter could never think of the loss of his land and goods as anything but a man-made calamity. He sometimes said it was partly his own fault, but he believed steadfastly that his position had been brought about by other people. He did not blame Captain John to the same extent that he blamed others, however. Captain John had always treated him fairly, and had done more for him than any other man. When Jeeter had overbought at the stores in Fuller, Captain John let him continue, and he never put a limit to the credit allowed. But the end soon came. There was no longer any profit in raising cotton under the Captain's antiquated system, and he abandoned the farm and moved to Augusta. Rather than attempt to show his tenants how to conform to the newer and more economical methods of modern agriculture, which he thought would have been an impossible task from the start, he sold the stock and implements and moved away. An intelligent employment of his land, stocks, and implements would have enabled Jeeter, and scores of others who had become dependent upon Captain John, to raise crops for food, and crops to be sold at a profit. Co-operative and corporate farming would have saved them all.

Jeeter was now reduced to painful poverty. His means of livelihood had been taken away, and he was slowly starving.

The entire section of land around him had originally been owned by Jeeter's grandfather. Seventy-five years before, it had been the most desirable soil in the entire west-central part of Georgia. His grandfather had cleared the greater part of the plantation for the production of tobacco. The soil at that time was better suited to the cultivation of tobacco than to that of any other crop. It was a sandy loam, and the ridge was high and dry. Hundreds of tumbled-down tobacco barns, chinked with clay, could still be found on what was left of the plantation; some of them were still standing, but most of them were rotted and fallen down.

The road on which Jeeter lived was the original tobacco road his grandfather had made. It was about fifteen miles long, and extended in a southeasterly direction from the foothills of the Piedmont, where the sand hills started, and ended on the bluffs at the river. The road had been used for the rolling of tobacco casks, large hogsheads in which the leaf had been packed after being cured and seasoned in the clay-chinked barns; thousands of hogsheads had been rolled along the crest of the ridge

63

which connected the chain of sand hills, and they had made a smooth firm road the entire distance of fifteen miles. Sometimes the casks had been pushed by gangs of negroes to the river steamboats, other times they were pulled by teams of mules; but always the crest of the ridge was followed, because when off it the hogsheads would have rolled downhill into the creeks which ran parallel with the road to the river, and once wet, the leaf would have been ruined and worthless.

After seventy-five years the tobacco road still remained, and while in many places it was beginning to show signs of washing away, its depressions and hollows had made a permanent contour that would remain as long as the sand hills. There were scores of tobacco roads on the western side of the Savannah Valley, some only a mile or so long, others extending as far back as twenty-five or thirty miles into the foothills of the Piedmont. Any one walking cross-country would more than likely find as many as six or eight in a day's hike. The region, topographically, was like a palm leaf; the Savannah was the stem, large at the bottom and gradually spreading out into veins at the top. On the side of the valley the creeks ran down like the depressions in the palm leaf, while between them lay the ridges of sand hills, like seams, and on the crests of the ridges were the tobacco roads.

Jeeter's father had inherited about one-half of the original Lester plantation, and approximately half of that had quickly slipped through his fingers. He could not pay the taxes, to begin with, and much of it had been sold to satisfy the county's claims from year to year. The remainder he farmed the best he could. He raised cotton exclusively, but because of the sandy loam he found it necessary to use more and more fertilizer each year. The loose sandy soil would not hold the guano during the hard summer rains, and it was washed away before the roots of the plants could utilize it.

64

By the time Jeeter was old enough to work in the fields, the land had become such a great item of expense that most of it was allowed to grow up into pines. The soil had become depleted by the constant raising of cotton year after year, and it was impossible to secure a yield of more than a quarter of a bale to the acre. More and more guano was poured into the fields, and faster and faster was it washed away through the loose sandy soil before the cotton plants were able to reach it.

When his father died, what was left of the Lester lands and debts was willed to Jeeter. The first thing that happened was the foreclosure of the mortgage. In order to satisfy the creditors, all the timber was cut, and another large portion of the land was sold. Two years later Jeeter found himself so heavily in debt that he did not own a single acre of land, or even a tenant house, after the claims had been settled. The man who purchased the farm at the sheriff's sale was Captain John Harmon. Captain John allowed Jeeter and his family to live in one of the houses, and to work for him on shares. That was ten years before the World War.

From that time forward, Jeeter had sunk each year into a poverty more bitter than that of the year before. The culmination had apparently been reached when Captain John sold the mules and other stock and moved to Augusta. There was then to be no more two-thirds' share of a year's labor coming to Jeeter, and there was never again to be credit for food and snuff and other necessities at the stores in Fuller. With him, Captain John took his credit. Jeeter did not know what to do. Without snuff and food, life seemed not worth living any longer.

By that time, most of the children had left home and gone to Augusta and elsewhere. Jeeter did not know where all of them were now.

There had been seventeen children born to Ada and him. Five had died, and the twelve living were scattered

65

in all directions. Only Ellie May and Dude were still at home; Pearl was only two miles away, but she never came to the house to see Jeeter and Ada, and they had never been to see her. The children who had died were buried in different parts of the farm. The land had been plowed over since their deaths, and as the graves were unmarked, no one would have known where to look for them if he had wanted to find them.

With the exception of Dude and Ellie May, all the children were married. Jeeter thought he knew where Tom was, but he was not certain. He had heard in the stores in Fuller that Tom, who was the oldest boy, was running a cross-tie camp in the next county at a place about twenty miles away.

Nobody had the slightest idea where most of the others were, nor if all of them were still living. Lizzie Belle had been the last one to leave home. She had gone away several years before, saying she was going to work in a cotton mill across the river from Augusta. There were ten or more cotton mills in Horsecreek Valley, but she had not said which one she was going to work in. Jeeter had been told that she was still there, and that she was married and had seven children already. He did not know if it was true or not, because neither he nor Ada ever received a letter.

There were times when Jeeter became lonesome without all his children around him, and he wished some of them would come back to see him, or write letters. He wondered then, too, if it were possible that they had sent him letters he had not received. There was no rural delivery route on the tobacco road, and he did not have a mail box; but he had said several times that he was some day going to the post-office in Fuller to ask if there was a letter for him from Lizzie Belle or Clara or Tom, or any of the others. He knew he would have to get somebody to read the letters to him if he did hear from them, because nei-

66

ther he nor Ada had ever learned to read. He had been in Fuller hundreds of times since he first thought of asking at the post-office for a letter, but he had not yet got around to making inquiry there.

Some day he hoped to be able to get over to Burke County and see Tom. He had been planning a trip over there for several years, but first it was the old automobile that had prevented him from getting started, then it was bad weather and muddy roads that held him back.

The trip to see Tom had been planned for two purposes; he wanted to see his son, of course, and to talk to him, but his main object in going was because he believed Tom would give him some money regularly when he found out how poor he was and how badly he and Ada needed snuff and food. From the things Jeeter had heard in the stores in Fuller, he knew Tom could afford to give him a few dollars every week. The people said that Tom owned fifty or sixty mules, and twice that many oxen, and that he received a lot of money for the cross-ties he sold the railroad. Jeeter had heard that several times in Fuller, and he knew it must be true. He could not believe that Tom would refuse to help him and Ada when he told his son how poor they were. Now that winter was passing, Jeeter hoped to be able to make the trip some time that summer. The roads would not be muddy then, and the days would be much longer.

The passing of winter and the slow growth of early spring had its usual effect on Jeeter. The warm late February days had kindled in him once more the desire to farm the land. Each year at that season he made a new effort to break the ground and to find means of buying seed-cotton and guano on credit from the merchants in Fuller. His attempts had always ended in the refusal of anybody to give him a dime's worth of credit. However, he burned a field here and a field there on the farm each spring, getting the growth of broom-sedge off the land so it would be ready to plow in case some one did lend him a mule and give him a little seed-cotton and guano. Each year for the past six or seven it had been the same.

There was an inherited love of the land in Jeeter that all his disastrous experiences with farming had failed to take away. He had lived his whole life there on a small remnant of the Lester plantation, and while he realized it was not his legally, he felt that he would die if he had to move away from it. He would not even consider going elsewhere to live, even though he were offered a chance to work another man's farm on shares. Even to move to Augusta and work in the cotton mills would be impossible for him. The restless movement of the other tenant farmers to the mills had never had any effect on Jeeter. Working in cotton mills might be all right for some people, he said, but as for him, he would rather die of starvation than leave the land. In seven years his views of the subject had not been altered; and if anything, he was more determined than ever to remain where he was at all cost.

When Lizzie Belle left, Ada had said she wanted to move to Augusta, too; but Jeeter would not listen to her argument. There had never been a time when he wanted to leave the land and live in a mill village.

"City ways ain't God-given," Jeeter had said, shaking his head. "It wasn't intended for a man with the smell of the land in him to live in a mill in Augusta. Maybe it's all right for some people to do that, but God never meant for me to do it. He put me on the land to start with, and I ain't leaving it. I'd feel just like a chicken with my head cut off living shut up in a mill all the time."

"You talk like an old fool," Ada had said angrily. "It's a whole lot better to live in the mills than it is to stay out here on the tobacco road and starve to death. Up there I could get me all the snuff I needed. Down here I ain't never got enough to calm me."

"God is aiming to provide for us," he had answered her.

68

"I'm getting ready right now to receive His bounty. I expect it to come most any time now. He won't let us stay here and starve. He'll send us some snuff and rations pretty soon. I been a God-fearing man all my life, and He ain't going to let me suffer no more."

"You just sit there and see! This time ten years from now you'll be just like you is now, if you live that long. Even the children has got more sense that you has— didn't they go off and work in the mills as soon as they was big enough? They had better sense than to sit here and wait for you to put food in their empty mouths and bellies. They knowed you'd never do nothing about it, except talk. If I wasn't so old, I'd go up to the mills right now and make me some money."

"The Lord sends me every misery He can think of just to try my soul. He must be aiming to do something powerful big for me, because He sure tests me hard. I reckon He figures if I can put up with my own people I can stand to fight back at the devil."

"Humph!" Ada had said. "If He don't hurry up and do something about it, it will be too late. My poor stomach gives me a powerful pain all day long when I ain't got the snuff to calm it."

CHAPTER VIII

THERE was nothing Jeeter could find to do in the sand hills that would pay him even a few cents a day for his labor. There were no farmers within twenty miles who hired help, because practically all of them were in Jeeter's condition, some of them in an even worse one; nor were there any lumber mills or turpentine stills anywhere near the tobacco road that would employ him. The only job in the surrounding country was the one at the coal chute, and Lov had held it since the Augusta and Georgia Southern Railroad was first built. Even if Jeeter could have taken the job away from Lov, the work would have been too hard for him to do. Filling the big iron scoops all day long and rolling them to the edge of the structure where they were dumped into the engine tenders, required a strong back and stronger arms. Lov could do the work, because he had become accustomed to doing it. For Jeeter to attempt such hard labor in the weakened condition he was in would have been foolish even if the railroad would have hired him.

The hope that he would find Tom was Jeeter's sustaining strength. Behind his hopeful belief that Tom would give him some money lay his fear of dying without a suit of clothes to be buried in. He had developed a growing horror of dying in overalls.

Ada, too, talked a lot about getting clothes to die in. She wanted a silk dress, and it mattered little to her whether the color was red or black, so long as it was stylish in length. Ada had a dress she had been keeping several years to die in, but she was constantly worried for fear that the dress might not be of the correct length. One year it was stylish to have dresses one length, and the next year they were mysteriously lengthened or shortened several inches. It had been impossible for her to keep up with the changes; consequently, even though she had a dress put away, she still tried to make Jeeter promise to buy her a new one that would be in style and in keeping with the times when she should die.

Ada believed she would die almost any day. She was usually surprised to wake up in the morning and discover that she was still alive. The pellagra that was slowly squeezing the life from her emaciated body was a lingering death. The old grandmother had pellagra, too, but somehow she would not die. Her frail body struggled day after day with the disease; but except for the slow withering of her skin and flesh no one was able to say when she would die. She weighed only seventy-two pounds now; once she had been a large woman, and she had weighed two hundred pounds twenty years before. Jeeter was angry with her because she persisted in living, and he would not let her have any food when he could keep her from eating it. However, she had learned now to find her own means of sustenance, such as it was. How she did it, no one knew. Sometimes she would boil leaves and roots, at other times she would eat wild grass and flowers in the fields.

Jeeter had already given implicit instructions regarding his own burial. He had impressed upon both Ada and Lov the importance and necessity of carrying out his plans. He expected to outlive Ada; but in case he should be killed in his automobile, he had made her promise to buy him a suit of clothes. If that was impossible, she was to go to Fuller and ask some of the merchants to give her an old suit for him. Lov, too, had had to swear that he would see that Jeeter was buried in a suit of clothes instead of in overalls.

But there was another thing connected with his death that was of equal importance.

Jeeter had a horror of rats. That was strange, because he had lived with them around him all his life, and he knew their ways almost as well as he did those of men. His reason for hating rats was because of an incident that had happened when his father died while Jeeter was a young man.

The older Lester had died in the same house Jeeter now occupied, and he was buried on the following day. That night, while Jeeter and the other men were sitting up with the body, some one had suggested that they all go to Fuller and get some Coca-Colas and tobacco. They were to sit up all night, and they had felt the need of something to drink and something to smoke. As all of the men, including Jeeter, had wanted to go to Fuller, they had put the body in the corn-crib and locked the door. The crib was the only place on the farm where anything could be locked up and found intact later. Negroes and white men had a habit of coming by the Lester house during the night and carrying away anything that had been left unprotected. None of the doors of the house had locks on them, but the crib door did have a lock. The men had placed the body inside, locked the door and put the key away, and had driven to Fuller for the Coca-Colas and tobacco.

They returned to the house about three or four hours later. As soon as the mules were unhitched from the buggies and tied to the wagon wheels for the rest of the night, the men unlocked the crib door, lifted out the wooden box, and carried it back into the house. The remainder of the night was spent in watching the casket, drinking Coca-Colas, and smoking and chewing tobacco.

The following afternoon at the funeral, just as the casket was about to be lowered into the grave, the top was lifted off in order that the family and friends might take a last look at the deceased. The lid was turned back, and just as it was fully open, a large corn-crib rat jumped out and disappeared in the woods. Nobody knew how the rat had got inside until some one found a hole in the bottom of the wooden box where the rat had gnawed through while it was locked in the crib.

One by one the people filed past the casket, and each time it became the next person's turn to look at the body, a strange look came over his face. Some of the women giggled, and the men grinned at each other. Jeeter ran to the side of the box and saw what had happened. The rat had eaten away nearly all of the left side of his father's face and neck. Jeeter closed the lid and had the box lowered into the grave immediately. He had never forgotten that day.

Now that the time was coming when he would soon die, Jeeter had become more insistent than ever that his body was not to be put into a corn-crib or left where the rats could reach it. Lov had promised faithfully to see that the rats did not get to him before he was buried.

"You've got to swear to me you won't let me be left in the box where the rats can get me," Jeeter had said dozens of times. "I declare before the good Lord, Lov, that ain't a fit way to treat the dead. I've regretted my own father's circumstance every day since that happened, and I declare before the Lord, I sure don't want that thing to happen to me when I'm dead and can't do nothing about it."

"You don't need to worry none," Lov had said. "I'll dig a hole and put you in it right after you're gone. I won't wait for the next day, even. I'll put you in the ground the

73

same hour you die, almost. I'll take care of your body. Don't you worry none."

"Just don't put the coffin in that durn corn-crib, Lov, no matter what else you do. There ain't no rats staying in there now since I ain't had corn in it for nearly five years, but they take trips back here every once in a while from the place they're staying at now just to make sure there ain't been no corn put in it. Before they left they et up mule collars and everything else they could get hold of, they was that mad at me for not putting corn in there for them. I used to bust them on the head with sticks, but that didn't stop them from coming back every once in a while. I was in there not so long ago getting me some corn cobs and one of them bit my leg before I could get out. They have sure got it in good and heavy for me, because I don't put no corn in there for them to eat up."

Ada, too, had promised Jeeter to see that his body would not be left exposed to the rats that he hated so much. But Jeeter did not worry her as much as he did Lov, because he believed he would out-live her by several years.

Ada herself looked as if she might die before Jeeter did. Her teeth had all dropped out; she had dipped snuff since she was eight years old. Her teeth had not lasted very long after she was married. Her one concern, besides the constant desire for more snuff, was with her own death. The thought that she might not have a stylish dress when she died was bothering her night and day. She did not trust Jeeter any too much to furnish it when the time came; that was the reason she kept the old dress put away to be used in case a more up-to-date one was not bought for her.

"If I could find out where my daughters was living, maybe they would help me get a stylish dress to die in," she had said. "Lizzie Belle used to love her old Ma a lot. I know she'd help me get one if I could find out where she

74

is at. And Clara might help some, too. She used to tell me how pretty I looked when I combed my hair of mornings and put on a clean apron and sunbonnet. I don't know if the others would want to help none or not. It's been such a long time since I saw the rest of them I've just about forgot what they was like. Seems like I can't recall all their names even, sometimes."

"Lizzie Belle might be making a lot of money over in the mills," Jeeter had said. "Maybe if we was to find her and ask her about it, she might come some time and bring us a little money. I know Bailey would bring us some snuff and rations if I knowed where to find him. Bailey was just about the best of all the boys. He was good to me even when he was just a little boy. He was never stealing all the molasses we had saving for supper, like the rest of them. I expect maybe he's got to be a pretty big merchant somewheres by now. He always said he was going to make a lot of money so he wouldn't have to go barefooted in the winter-time like Tom and Clara did when they went away."

Ada talked to Jeeter whenever the subject was that of their children away from home. It seemed as if she were not interested enough in other things to talk about them any more. She answered Jeeter's questions most of the time, and she scolded him when there was nothing in the house to eat. The rest of the time she had very little to say. But whenever Bailey's name, or Lizzie Belle's, or Clara's, or Walker's, or any of the children's was mentioned, she lost the hollow look in her eyes and wanted to talk about them for the rest of the day. None of the children who had left home had ever been back to visit, nor had they ever sent a message. Because Ada and Jeeter had never received one, they believed that all of the children were alive. There was no way of knowing whether they were dead or not.

"I'm going over to Burke County and see Tom,"

Jeeter had told Ada. "I've made up my mind that I'll go over there and see him before I die. Everybody in Fuller tells me he's hauling cross-ties out of the camp by the wagon load day and night. They say he's got a whopping big cross-tie camp over there. From what people say about him, I reckon he's a powerful rich man now. He sure ought to give me some money. Though it sometimes looks like a rich man will never help the poor; whereas the poor people will give away everything they has to help somebody who ain't got nothing. That's how it looks to me. Don't seem like it ought to be that way, but I reckon the rich ain't got no time to fool with us poor folks."

"When you see Tom, tell him that his old Ma would like powerful much to see him. You tell him that I said he was near about the best of the whole seventeen. Clara and Lizzie Belle was about the best, I reckon; but Tom and Bailey led the boys when it came to being good children. You tell Tom I said he was the best of them, and maybe he'll send me some money for a stylish dress."

"Pearl is the prettiest," Jeeter said. "Ain't none of the other gals got pretty yellow hair like she has. Nor them pale blue eyes, neither. She's the first Lester I ever saw who had yellow hair. It's funny about her having it, ain't it, Ada?"

"Pearl is my favorite, I reckon," Ada said. "I wish she would come to see me sometimes. I ain't seen her since she left last summer to get married to Lov."

"I'm going to tell Tom he ought to give me some money," Jeeter said. "The folks in Fuller say he's a powerful rich man now."

"You better not forget to mention to him that his old Ma sure would like for him to get her a stylish dress to die in. I know he won't stand back with a little of his money for a little thing like that."

"I'm going to mention it to him when I see him, but I

76

don't know how he'll take it. I expect he's got a wife and a raft of children to provide for. Maybe he'll give it to me, though."

"Reckon Tom has got some children?"

"Maybe some."

"I sure would like to see them. I know I must have a whole lot of grandchildren somewhere. I'm bound to have, with all them boys and girls off from home. If I could see Tom maybe I wouldn't mind it so bad that I can't see the rest of them. I just know I ought to have grandchildren somewhere in the country."

"Lizzie Belle and Clara has got a raft of children, I reckon. They was always talking about having them. And they say over in Fuller that Lizzie Belle has got a lot of them. I don't know how other folks know more about such things than I do. Looks like I ought to be the one who knows the most about my children."

"Maybe you could get Tom to bring his children over here for me to see. You tell him I want to see my grandchildren, and maybe he'll consent to bring them."

Ada had talked several times about Tom bringing his children to see her. Every time Jeeter said anything about going over to Burke County where Tom's cross-tie camp was, she reminded him not to forget to tell Tom what she had said. But from year to year, as Jeeter failed to start, she had become less inclined to talk about the possibility of seeing any of the grandchildren. Jeeter could not get started. He would say he was going the next day, but he always put off the trip at the last minute.

Jeeter made a false start somewhere nearly every day. He was going to Fuller, or he was going to McCoy, or he was going to Augusta; but he never went when he said he would. If he told Ada at night that he was going to McCoy early the next morning, he would decide at the last minute to go to Fuller or Augusta instead. Usually he would have to stop and walk out over the old cotton fields and look at the tall brown broom-sedge, and that made him think about something else. When he did walk out into the sedge, the chances were that he would lie down and take a nap. It was a wonder how he ever got the wood cut that he hauled to Augusta. Sometimes it took him a whole week to cut enough blackjack for a load.

Just then it was the beginning of the new season that was causing him to change his mind so frequently. The smell of the burning broom-sedge and pine undergrowth was in the air every day now. Some of the land was even being broken away off in the distance, and he could detect the aroma of freshly turned earth miles away. The smell of newly turned earth, that others were never conscious of, reached Jeeter's nostrils with a more pungent odor than any one else could ever detect in the air. That made him want to go out right away and burn over the old cotton fields and plant a crop. Other men were doing that all around him, but even if he succeeded in borrowing a mule, Jeeter did not know where to begin begging for credit to buy seed-cotton and guano. The merchants in Fuller had heard his plea so many times that they knew what he was going to ask for as soon as he walked in the door, and before he could say the first word they were shaking their heads and going back where he could not follow them. He did not know what to do about it.

Jeeter postponed nearly everything a man could think of, but when it came to plowing the land and planting cotton, he was as persistent as any man could be about such things. He started out each day with his enthusiasm at fever pitch, and by night he was still as determined as ever to find a mule he could borrow and a merchant who would give him credit for seed-cotton and guano.

CHAPTER IX

THE sun had been up only half an hour when Bessie reached the Lester house on the morning after her sudden departure. She had said then that she was going home to ask God to let her marry Dude. Jeeter had not expected her to come back for several days.

No one was in sight as she crossed the yard and ran through the front door calling Dude.

"Dude—you Dude! Where is you, Dude?" she called.

Jeeter was just getting out of bed when he first heard her; she ran into the bedroom while he sat on a chair pulling on his shoes.

"What you want with Dude, Bessie?" he asked sleepily. "What you want Dude for?"

Bessie ran around the room looking into the beds. There were three beds in which all the Lesters slept. Ada and Jeeter used one of them, Ellie May and the grandmother another, and Dude slept alone.

Ellie May sat up in bed, awakened by the disturbance, and rubbed her eyes. Bessie jerked back the quilts on Dude's bed, and ran into the next room where the roof had fallen in. It was the other bedroom, the room where most of the children had formerly slept, and it had been deserted because one section of the roof had rotted away. It was filled with plunder.

79

Bessie came back and looked under Ada's bed.

"What you want with Dude this time of day, Bessie?" Jeeter asked.

She still did not stop to answer Jeeter's questions. She ran through the kitchen calling Dude at the top of her voice.

As soon as he could lace his shoes and put on his jumper, Jeeter followed her out into the backyard. His drooping black felt hat was on his head, because his hat was the first thing he put on in the morning and the last he took off at night.

Dude was drawing a bucket of water at the well, and Bessie reached him before he could tip the bucket and get a drink. She threw her arms around his neck and kissed his face excitedly. Dude fought back at first, but as soon as he saw it was Bessie he smiled at her and put his arms around her waist.

Jeeter went closer and watched them. Presently Bessie took a side-comb from her head and began combing Dude's stiff black hair and smoothing it down with the palms of her hands. Dude's hair was coarse and bristly, and it stood straight on its ends no matter how much it was combed and brushed. Sometimes he could manage to make it lie down for a few minutes by sousing his head in a pan of water and then combing it hurriedly; but as soon as the water began to dry, the hair would stand straight up again as if it were attached to springs. Dude's hair was as wiry as hog-bristles.

"I never seen a woman preacher carry-on over a young sapling like that before," Jeeter said. "What you want to do that to Dude for, Bessie? You and him is hugging and rubbing of the other just like you was yesterday on the front porch."

Bessie smiled at Dude and Jeeter. She leaned against the well-stand and tucked up her hair. She had not waited that morning to pin it up.

80

"Me and Dude is going to get married," she said. "The Lord told me to do it. I asked Him about it, and he said, 'Sister Bessie, Dude Lester is the man I want you to mate. Get up early in the morning and go up to the Lester place and marry Dude the first thing.' That's what He said to me last night, the very words I heard with my own ears while I was praying about it in bed. So when the sun came up, I got out of bed and ran up here as fast as I could, because the Lord don't like to be kept waiting for His plans to be carried out. He wants me to marry Dude right now."

Dude looked around nervously as if he was thinking of trying to run off to the woods and hide. He had forgotten how anxious he had been to go home with Bessie the evening before when she first mentioned marriage.

"You hear that, Dude?" Jeeter said. "What you think about doing it with Sister Bessie?"

"Shucks," he said. "I couldn't do that."

"Why can't you do that?" Jeeter demanded. "What's ailing you? Ain't you man enough yet?"

"Maybe I is, and maybe I ain't. I'd be scared to do that with her."

"Why, Dude," his father said, "that ain't nothing to be afraid about. Bessie ain't going to hurt you. She knows how to treat you. Sister Bessie, there, has been married before. She's a widow-woman now. She knows all about how to treat men."

"I wouldn't hurt you none, Dude," she said, putting her arm around his neck and drawing his arms tighter around her waist. "There ain't nothing to be scared of. I'm just like your sister, Ellie May, and your Ma. Women don't scare their menfolks none. You'll like being married to me, because I know how to treat men fine."

Ada elbowed her way past Jeeter and Dude. She had not waited to plait her hair when she heard what Bessie wanted. She stood beside Dude and Bessie, with her hair

81

divided over the front of her shoulders, plaiting one side and tying a string around the end, and then beginning on the other braid. She was as excited as Bessie was.

"Bessie," she said, "you'll have to make Dude wash his feet every once in a while, because if you don't he'll dirty-up your quilts. Sometimes he don't wash himself all winter long, and the quilts get that dirty you don't know how to go about the cleaning of them. Dude is just careless like his Pa. I had the hardest time learning him to wear his socks in the bed, because it was the only way I could keep the quilts clean. He would never wash himself. I reckon Dude is just going on the same way his Pa done, so maybe you had better make Dude wear his socks, too."

Ellie May had come out of the house and was standing behind a chinaberry tree in order to hear and see what was taking place beside the well-stand. The grandmother was in the yard too; she was peering from behind the corner of the house lest any one should see her and make her go away.

"Maybe you and Dude will help get me a stylish dress," Ada suggested shyly. "You and him know how bad I want a dress of the right length to die in. I've long ago give up waiting for Jeeter to get me one. He ain't going to do it in time."

All of them stood by the well looking at each other. When Jeeter caught Dude's eye, Dude hung his head and looked at the ground. He did not know what to think about it. He wanted to get married, but he was afraid of Bessie. She was nearly twenty-five years older than he was.

"Do you know what I'm going to do, Jeeter?" Bessie asked.

"What?" Jeeter said.

"I'm going to buy me a new automobile!"

"A new automobile?"

82

"A brand-new one. I'm going to Fuller right now and get it."

"A brand-new one?" Jeeter said unbelievingly. "A sure-enough brand-new automobile?"

Dude's mouth dropped open, and his eyes glistened.

"What you going to buy it with, Bessie?" Jeeter asked. "Is you got money?"

"I've got eight hundred dollars to pay for it with. My former husband left me that money when he died. He had it in insurance, and when he died I got it and put it in the bank in Augusta. I aimed to use it in carrying on the prayer and preaching my former husband used to like so much. I always did want a brand-new automobile."

"When you going to buy a new automobile?" Jeeter asked.

"Right now—to-day. I'm going over to Fuller and get it right now. Me and Dude's going to use it to travel all over the country preaching and praying."

"Can I drive it?" Dude asked.

"That's what I'm buying it for, Dude. I'm getting it for you to drive us around in when we take a notion to go somewheres."

"When is you and Dude going to do all this riding around and praying and preaching?" Jeeter said. "Is you going to get married before or after?"

"Right away," she said. "We'll walk over to Fuller right now and buy the new automobile, and then ride up to the courthouse and get married."

"Is you going to get leave of the county to get married?" he asked doubtfully. "Or is you just going to live along without it?"

"I'm going to get the license for marrying," she said.

"That costs about two dollars," Jeeter reminded. "Is you got two dollars? Dude ain't. Dude, he ain't got nothing."

"I ain't asking Dude for one penny of money. I'll attend to that part myself. I've got eight hundred dollars in

83

the bank, and some more besides. I saved my money for something just like this to happen. I've been looking for it to happen all along."

Dude had been dropping pebbles into the well for the past few minutes. Suddenly he stopped and looked at Bessie. He looked straight into her face, and the sight of the two cavernous round nostrils brought a smile to his lips. He had looked at her nose before, but this time the holes seemed to be larger and rounder than ever. It was more like looking down into a double-barrel shotgun than ever before. He could not keep from laughing.

"What you laughing at, Dude?" she asked, frowning.

"At them two holes in your nose," he said. "I ain't never seen nobody with all the top of her nose gone away like that before."

Bessie's face turned white. She hung her head in an effort to hide her exposed nostrils as much as possible. She was sensitive about her appearance, but she knew of no way to remedy her nose. She had been born without a bone in it, and after nearly forty years it had still not developed. She put her hand over her face.

"I'm ashamed of you, Dude," she said, wiping the tears from the corners of her eyes. "You know I can't help the way I look. I been like that ever since I can remember. Won't no nose grow on me, I reckon."

Dude dug the toes of his shoes in the sand and tried not to laugh. But almost as suddenly as he had first looked at Bessie's face and broken into a smile, he stopped and scowled meanly at himself. It was the remembrance of the new automobile that made him stop laughing at Bessie. If she was going to buy a brand-new car, he did not care how she looked. It would have been all right with him if she had had a harelip like Ellie May's, now that he could ride all he wanted to. He had never driven a new motor car, and that was something he wanted to do more than anything else he could think of.

84

"I didn't mean no harm," he said uneasily. "Honest to God, I didn't. I don't give a damn how your nose looks."

Bessie smiled again, and put her arms around his waist. She looked up at him again, her face so close to his that he could feel her breath. He had to stop trying to see down into her nose, because it hurt his eyes, and made them ache, to focus them on an object only a few inches away. Her nostrils were only a dark blur on her face when they were standing so close together.

"Can I drive the new automobile, sure enough?" he asked again, hoping he had not made her change her mind. "Is you going to let me drive it?"

"That's why I'm getting it, Dude. I'm getting it for you to drive all over the country in. Me and you is going to get married, and we can ride all the time if we want to. I won't stop you from going somewhere when you want to go. You can ride all the time."

"Will it have a horn on it?"

"I reckon it will. Don't all new automobiles come with horns all ready on them?"

"Maybe so," he said. "You be sure and find out if it's got one when you buy it, anyway. It won't be no good at all unless it's got a horn."

"Dude is pretty durn lucky," Jeeter said. "I didn't get a durn thing when I married Ada, there. She didn't have nothing but some old dresses of her own, and her people was that durn poor they had to eat meal and fat-back just like we do now. I didn't get nothing when I married her, except a mess of trouble."

Ada walked over to Bessie and laid her hand on Bessie's arm.

"Maybe if you got all that money, Bessie, you and Dude could buy me a jar of snuff in Fuller. Reckon you could do that for Dude's old Ma? Being that Dude is my boy, you ought to get me just a little jar of snuff, anyway. I'd sure be powerful pleased if you was to get three or

85

four jars while you was about it, though. Snuff drives away the pains in my poor stomach when I can't get nothing to eat."

"I been needing a new pair of overalls for the longest time, Bessie," Jeeter said. "I declare, I'm almost scared to go a far piece from the house any more, because I don't know but what my clothes will drop right off of me some time when I ain't noticing. If you could get me a new pair in Fuller, I'd be powerful pleased."

Bessie led Dude away from the well. They walked around the house, and when nobody was looking, she stood behind him and hugged him so hard he could not breathe until she released him.

"What you doing that to me for?" he said. "I ain't never had that done to me before."

"Me and you is going to get married, Dude. Don't you know that?"

He walked around behind her, looked at the back of her head, and came back in front again.

"When is you going to get a new automobile?" he asked.

"Right away, Dude. We're going to Fuller right now and get it."

Dude was more excited over the prospect of driving a new automobile than he had ever been about anything in his whole life. The automobiles he had seen had all been old ones like Jeeter's, except the ones the rich people in Augusta drove. He could not make himself believe that he was actually going to drive one like those he had seen in the city. He wanted to start for Fuller without another minute's delay.

"Come on," he said. "We ain't got no time to lose."

"Ain't you glad we is going to get married, though?" she said. "It's going to be real nice, ain't it, Dude?"

The rest of the Lesters had followed them to the front yard, and they stood by the corner of the house waiting to

86

see Dude and Bessie leave for Fuller. Ellie May followed them down the road for about half a mile before she turned around and came back to the house.

Dude walked in front, and Bessie followed him several yards behind. When they reached the top of the first sand hill, they stopped and looked back at the Lester house to see if Ada and Jeeter were watching them. Bessie waved her hand until Dude told her to hurry up so they could get to Fuller.

The long walk to Fuller took them nearly two hours, because Bessie had to stop several times and rest beside the road. The sun was hot by that time, as it was nearly ten o'clock when they left the Lester place; and it was difficult walking through the deep sand, especially for Bessie. In some places the sand was a foot deep, and her feet sank down so far that the sand ran down her shoe tops. Dude would never sit down and wait for Bessie to get ready to start walking again. He waited several hundred feet away, urging her to hurry.

Dude had started out walking slowly enough for Bessie to keep up with him; but as they got closer to Fuller, Dude could not hold himself back. He ran ahead several hundred yards, and then had to walk back to meet Bessie. He would have gone on to town without her, but he did not know what to do when he got there. He was afraid, too, that if he got out of Bessie's sight she might turn around and go back without buying the new automobile.

Neither of them talked the whole time. Bessie hummed a hymn to herself, occasionally raising a note to the shrill pitch she liked so much, but she did not try to talk to Dude. They were too engrossed in their own thoughts to talk.

CHAPTER X

DUDE waited outside the garage and looked at the new automobile on display in the show window. Bessie had gone inside. Dude had said he would stay on the street and look through the window a while.

Bessie waited in the middle of the floor several minutes before any one came out of the back room to ask what she wanted. Presently a salesman walked over to her and asked her if she wanted anything. He noticed that there was something unusual about her nose the moment he first saw her.

"I came to buy a new Ford," she said.

The salesman was so busy looking down into her nostrils that he had to ask her to repeat what she said.

"I came to buy a new Ford."

"Have you got any money?"

He glanced around to see if any of the other men were in the room. He wanted them to take a good look at Bessie's nose.

"I've got enough to buy a new automobile if it don't cost more than eight hundred dollars."

He looked up into her eyes for the first time. It was hard to believe from her appearance that she had as much as a penny.

"How'd you get it?" he said.

"The Lord provides for me. He always provides for His children."

"He ain't never sent me nothing, and I been here thirty years now. You must be on the inside some way."

The salesman laughed at what he had said, and looked down into Bessie's nostrils again.

"That's because you don't put your trust in the Lord."

"You ain't got that much money sure enough, have you?"

Bessie took the check-book from her skirt pocket and showed it to him. While he was looking at the name of the bank and the balance to her account tabulated on the stub, she walked to the door and motioned to Dude to come inside.

"Who's that?" the man said. "Is he your kid?"

"That's Dude Lester. Everybody's heard of the Lesters on the tobacco road. Me and Dude is going to get married to-day. As soon as we can get the new automobile we're going to ride around to the courthouse and get leave to marry."

The salesman shoved the check-book into her hands, and ran to the door of the office.

"Come here quick, Harry!" he said. "I got a real sight to show you."

An older man came out of the office and walked over to where Bessie and the salesman stood.

"What's up?" he said, glancing from one to the other.

"This woman here is going to marry that kid, Harry— what do you know about that! Have you ever seen anything like it before?"

The older man asked Dude how old he was.

Dude was about to tell him that he was sixteen when Bessie pushed him behind her.

"That's none of your business, how old he is. I want to buy a new automobile. That's what I came here for. I walked five miles this morning to get here, too."

89

The two men were whispering to each other when she had finished talking. The older one looked at her face, and when he saw the two large round holes in her nose, he stepped forward and tried to see down into her nostrils. Bessie covered her nose with her hand.

"Good God!" he said.

"Ain't it a sight, though?" the salesman said.

"Has she got any money?" Harry asked him. "Don't waste no time fooling with her if she ain't. There's a lot of them just like her who come in here from the country and never buy nothing."

"She's got a check-book on the Farmers' Bank in Augusta, and she said she's got eight hundred dollars in her account. The stub shows it, too."

"Better call them up and find out about it first," Harry said. "She might be telling the truth, and she might be lying. Some of them people out in the country do some tricky things sometimes. She might have found the check-book and filled it out herself."

They went back into the office talking about Bessie's nose, and closed the door. After the salesman had called the bank, they came out again where Bessie and Dude were waiting.

"How much do you want to pay for a car?" the salesman said.

"Eight hundred dollars," Bessie told him.

Harry nudged the salesman with his elbow.

"Now, this is a nice little job here," he said, leaning against the fender of a new touring model. "It's eight hundred dollars. You can drive it away to-day, if you want to. You won't have to wait for the tags. I'll get them for you some time next week. You can drive a new car anywhere in the State for seven days while you are waiting for the tags to come from Atlanta."

They winked at each other; every time they wanted to

put over a quick sale they told that lie about the registration laws.

Dude went to the car and blew the horn several times. The tone of it pleased him, and he grinned at Bessie.

"Do you like it, Dude?"

"Ain't nothing wrong with it," he said, blowing the horn again.

"We'll take that one," Bessie said, pointing at the car.

"Let's see your check-book," the other man said, jerking it out of Bessie's hand before she could give it to him.

He took the check-book, tore out a blank, and hastily filled it out for eight hundred dollars.

While the man was writing the check for Bessie to sign before she could change her mind or leave the garage, the salesman was again trying to look down into her nose. He had never seen anything like it before in all his life.

"Sign your name here," she was told.

"I always have to make my mark," she said.

"What's your name?"

"Sister Bessie Rice."

"You must be a woman preacher," the man said. "Ain't you one?"

"I preach and pray, both."

She touched the end of the pen while an "x" was crossed after her name on the check.

"The automobile's yours," she was told. "Is the boy going to drive it home for you?"

"Wait a minute," Bessie said. "I clear forgot about praying—let's all kneel down on the floor and have a little prayer before the trade is made."

"It's all over with now," one of them said.

"No it ain't, neither," Bessie insisted. "It ain't over till the Lord sends his blessings on it."

The two men laughed at her insistence, but Bessie had already knelt down on the floor and Dude was getting

91

down on his knees beside the automobile. The two men stood behind her so they would not have to kneel on the floor.

"Dear God, we poor sinners kneel down in this garage to pray for a blessing on this new automobile trade, so You will like what me and Dude is doing. This new automobile is for me and Dude to ride around in and do the work You want done for You in this sinful country. You ought to make us not have wrecks with it, so we won't get hurt none. You don't want us to get killed, right when we're starting out to preach the gospel for You, do You? And these two men here who sold the new car to us need your blessing, too, so they can sell automobiles for the best good. They is sinful men just like all the rest of us, but I know they don't aim to be, and You ought to bless their work and show them how to sell people new automobiles for the best good, just like You would do if You was down here selling automobiles Yourself, in Fuller. That's all. Save us from the devil and make a place for us in heaven. Amen."

Dude was the first to get on his feet. He jumped up and blew the horn six or seven long blasts. The two men came around in front of Bessie, wiping the perspiration from their faces, and laughing at Dude and Bessie. They looked at her nose again until she put her hand over it.

Dude and Bessie got into the automobile and sat down. Dude blew the horn again several times.

"Wait a minute," the salesman said. "We'll have to roll it outside first and fill up the tank with gas. You can't drive it like it is now."

Bessie got out, but Dude refused to leave the horn and steering wheel. He sat where he was and guided the car through the door while the men pushed.

After the gasoline had been pumped into the tank, Dude started the engine and got ready to leave. Bessie got in again, sitting in the centre of the back seat.

"Where you going now?" the salesman asked Bessie. "To get married?"

"We're going around to the courthouse to get leave of the county," she said. "Then we'll get married."

The two men whispered to each other.

"Did you ever see a nose like that before, Harry?"

"Not when I was sober."

"Look at them two big round holes running down into her face—how does she keep it from raining down in there, you reckon?"

"I'll be damned if I know. Maybe she puts cork stoppers in them to keep the water out. She would have to do something like that in a hard shower."

Bessie leaned over and prodded Dude.

"Drive off, Dude," she said. "Ain't no sense in staying here no more."

Dude put the car into gear and turned the gasoline on. Being unaccustomed to the new model, he did not know how to gauge the amount of gasoline, and the car jerked off so quickly that it almost lifted itself off the ground. The two men jumped out of the way just in time to keep from being hit by the fender.

Bessie showed Dude which way to turn to find the courthouse. When they reached it, Dude got out reluctantly and followed Bessie inside. He wanted to stay in the car and blow the horn, but Bessie said he had to go with her to get the license.

The Clerk's office was found at the end of the hall on the first floor, and they opened the door and went inside. There was a cardboard sign on the door that Bessie remembered seeing when she came there with her first husband.

"I want leave to get married to Dude," she stated.

The Clerk looked at her and spread out a blank on the table. He gave her a pen and motioned to her to fill it in with answers to the questions.

93

"You'll have to write it for me. I can't write the words down."

"Can't you write?" he asked. "Can't you sign your name?"

"I never learned how," she said.

He was about to say something, when he looked up and saw her nose. His eyes opened wider and wider.

"All right, I'll put it down for you. But it ain't my business to do that for you. You ought to do it yourself. I don't get paid for writing people's names for them."

"I'll be powerful much obliged if you will do it for me," she said.

"What's your name?"

"Sister Bessie Rice."

"You must be preacher Rice's widow, ain't you?"

"He was my former husband."

"Who are you going to marry, Sister Rice?"

"That's him back there by the door."

"Who?"

"Dude. His name is Dude Lester."

"You ain't going to marry him, are you?"

"That's what I came here to get leave of the county for. Me and him is going to get married."

"Who—that kid?" Is he the one who's going to marry you?"

"Dude said he would ———"

"That boy ain't old enough to marry yet, Sister Rice."

"Dude, he's sixteen."

"I can't give you a license—you'll have to wait a while and come back next year or so."

"Dear God," Bessie said, dropping to her knees on the floor, "this man says he won't give me leave to marry Dude. God, You've got to make him do it. You told me last night to marry Dude and make a preacher out of him, and You have got to see me through now. I'm all excited about getting married. If You don't make the

94

county give me leave to marry, I don't know what evil I might ———"

"Wait a minute!" the Clerk shouted. "Stop that praying! I'd rather give you the license than listen to that. Maybe we can do something about it."

Bessie got up smiling.

"I knowed the Lord would help me out," she said.

"Has that boy got the consent of his parents? He can't get married unless he's got the consent of both parents, according to the law for his age. What does he want to marry you for anyway? He's too young to marry an old woman like you. Come here, son ———"

"Don't you try to talk him out of it," Bessie said. "If you start that, I'll pray some more. God won't let you keep us from marrying."

"What do you mean by coming here to marry this old woman, son? You ought to wait and marry a girl when you grow up."

"I don't know," Dude said. "Bessie, there, brought me along with her."

"Well, I can't give you a license to marry," the Clerk said. "It's against the law for a boy under eighteen years old to marry without his parents' consent. And no amount of praying can change the law, neither. It's down on the books and it won't come off."

"Dear God," Bessie began again, "You ain't going to let this man put us off, is You? You know how much I been counting on marrying Dude. You ought not to let nothing stop ———"

"Wait a minute! Don't start that again!" the Clerk said. "Who are this boy's folks?"

"His Ma and Pa don't care," Bessie said. "They're glad of it. I talked to them both early this morning on the way down here to Fuller."

"What's his daddy's name?"

"Jeeter Lester is Dude's Pa, and I don't reckon you

95

would know his Ma if I was to call her name. Her name is Ada."

"Sure, I know Jeeter Lester, and I don't reckon he does care. Nor his wife, either. I had to give Lov Bensey a license to marry one of the young girls, because Jeeter said he wanted it done. She wasn't but twelve years old then either, and it was a shame to marry her so young. But it's in the law, and I had to do it. She was a pretty little girl. I never seen a girl before in all my life with such pretty yellow hair and blue eyes. Her eyes was exactly the same color as robins' eggs. I swear, she was one pretty sight to see."

"Dude is older than that," Bessie said. "Dude, he is sixteen."

"How old are you, Sister Rice? You didn't tell me your age."

"I don't have to tell you that, do I?" she said.

"That's the law. I can't give you the license if you don't state your age."

"Well—I was thirty-eight not so long back."

"How old are you now?"

"Thirty-nine, but I don't show it yet."

"Who's going to support you two?" he asked. "That boy can't make a man's wages yet."

"Is that in the law, too?"

"Well, no. The law doesn't require that question, but I thought I'd just like to know about it myself."

"The Lord will provide," Bessie said. "He always makes provision for His children."

"He don't take none too good care of me and mine," the Clerk said, "and I been a supporting member of the Fuller Baptist church since I was twenty years old, too. He don't do none too much for me."

"That's because you ain't got the right kind of religion," Bessie said. "The Baptists is sinners like all the rest, but my religion provides for me."

96

"What's the name of it?"

"It ain't got no regular name. I just call it 'Holy,' most of the time. I'm the only member of it now, but Dude is going to be one when we get married. He's going to be a preacher, too."

"You'll have to pay me two dollars for the license," he said, writing on the sheet of paper. "Have you got it?"

"I've got it right here. I don't see, though, why folks has to pay to get married. It's God's doings."

"There's something else I'm going to ask you. It's not required by law, and some clerks don't ask about it, but being a good Baptist I always feel like I ought to."

"What's it about?"

"Has either of you got any disease?"

"Not that I know about," she said. "Has you, Dude?"

"What's that?"

"Disease," the Clerk said again, pronouncing the word slowly. "Like pellagra and chicken-pox, or anything like that. Is there anything wrong with you, son?"

"I ain't got anything wrong with me that I know about," Dude said. "I don't know what that thing is, noway."

"You sure you haven't?" he asked Bessie. "Did your husband leave you with disease of any kind? What did he die of?"

"He died of age mostly, I reckon. He was well on to fifty when we was married."

"Has either one of you got venereal disease?"

"What's that?" Bessie asked.

"You know—" he said, "venereal disease. Maybe you call it sex trouble."

"I used to take a powerful number of bottles of Tanlac, but I ain't lately because I ain't had the money to buy them with."

"No, not that. What I'm talking about comes from women sleeping with men, sometimes."

97

"My former husband had mites on him pretty bad sometimes. I had to wash both him and me off with kerosene to get rid of them."

"No, not mites. Lots of people get those on them. It's something else—but I reckon you ain't got it, if you don't know what I'm talking about."

"What other things do you want to know?" Bessie said.

"That's all, I reckon. Now, you give me the two dollars."

Bessie handed him the two soiled and ragged one-dollar bills she had been gripping in her hand. She had several more in her skirt pocket, all of them rolled in a handkerchief and the ends tied together. It was all the money she had left, now that the eight hundred dollars had been paid for the new automobile.

"Well, I reckon you two will get along all right," the Clerk said. "Maybe you will, and maybe you won't."

"Is you a married man?" Bessie asked.

"I been married fifteen years or more. Why?"

"Well, I reckon you know how pleased me and Dude is to get married, then," she said. "All married folks know how it is to get married."

"It's all right at the beginning, but it don't keep up like that long. After you been married a year or two a man wants to go out and do it again all over, but it can't be done. The law puts a stop to it after the first time, unless your wife dies, or runs off, but that don't happen often enough to make it of any good."

"Me and Dude is going to stay together all the time, ain't we, Dude?"

Dude grinned, but he did not speak.

Bessie had the license in her hand, and she did not wait to hear the Clerk talk any more. She pulled Dude out of the room, and they left the courthouse and ran to the new automobile.

They got in to ride home. Dude blew the horn several

98

times before he started the motor, and again before he put the car into gear. Then he turned it around in the street and drove it out of Fuller towards the tobacco road.

Bessie sat erect on the back seat, holding the marriage license tight in both hands so the wind would not blow it away.

CHAPTER XI

THE Lesters heard Dude blowing the horn far down the tobacco road long before the new automobile came within sight, and they all ran to the farthest corner of the yard, and even out into the broom-sedge, to see Dude and Bessie arrive. Even the old grandmother was excited, and she waited behind a chinaberry tree to be among the first to see the new car.

"Here they come!" Jeeter shouted. "Just look at them! It's a brand-new automobile, all right— just look at that shiny black paint! Great-day-in-the-morning! Just look at them coming yonder!"

Dude was driving about twenty miles an hour, and he was so busy blowing the horn he forgot to slow down when he turned into the yard. The car jolted across the ditch, throwing Bessie against the top three or four times in quick succession, and breaking several leaves of the rear spring. Dude slowed down then, and the automobile rolled across the yard and came to a stop by the side of the house.

Jeeter was the first to reach the new motor car. He had run behind it while Dude was putting on the brakes, and he had held to the rear mudguard while trying to keep up with it. Ellie May and Ada were not far behind. The grandmother came as quickly as she could.

"I never seen a finer-looking automobile in all my days," Jeeter said. "It sure does make me happy again to see such a handsome machine. Don't you reckon you could take me for a little trip, Bessie? I sure would like to go off in it for a piece."

Bessie opened the door and got out. The first thing she did was to take the bottom of her skirt and rub the dust off of the front fenders.

"I reckon we can take you riding in it some time," she said. "When me and Dude gets back, you can go riding."

"Where is you and Dude going to, Bessie?"

"We're going to ride around like married folks," she said proudly. "When folks get married, they always like to take a little ride together somewhere."

Ada and Ellie May inspected the car with stifled admiration. Both of them then gathered up the bottoms of their skirts and shined the doors and fenders. The new automobile shone in the bright sun like a looking-glass when they had finished.

Dude climbed over the door and ordered his mother and sister away from the car.

"You and Ellie May will be ruining it," he said. "Don't put your hands on it and don't stand too close to it."

"Did you and Dude get married in Fuller?" Jeeter asked Bessie.

"Not all the way," she said. "I got leave of the county, however. It cost two dollars to do that little bit."

"Ain't you going to get a preacher to finish doing it?"

"I is not! Ain't I a preacher of the gospel? I'm going to do it myself. I wouldn't allow no Hard-shell Baptist to fool with us."

"I knowed you would do it the right way," Jeeter said. "You sure is a fine woman preacher, Sister Bessie."

Bessie moved towards the front porch, twisting the marriage license in her hands. Every one else was still looking at the new automobile. Ellie May and Ada stood at a safe distance so Dude would not run them away with a stick. The old grandmother had gone behind a chinaberry tree again, awed by the sight.

Dude walked around in a circle so he could see all sides of the car. He wanted to be certain that nobody put his hands on the car and dulled its lustre.

Jeeter sat down on his heels and admired it.

Bessie had gone half way up the front steps, and she was trying to attract Dude's attention. She coughed several times, scraped her feet on the boards, and rapped on the porch with her knuckles. Jeeter heard her, and he looked around to find out what she was doing.

"By God and by Jesus!" he said, jumping to his feet. "Now wasn't that just like a fool man?"

The others turned around and looked at Bessie. Ellie May giggled from behind a chinaberry tree.

"Ada," Jeeter said, "Sister Bessie is wanting to go in the house. You go show her in."

Ada went inside and threw open the blinds. She could be heard dragging chairs around the room and pushing the beds back into the corners.

"Didn't you and Dude stop off in the woods coming back from Fuller?" he asked Bessie.

"We was in a hurry to get back here," she said. "I mentioned it, sort of, to Dude, but he was blowing the horn so much he couldn't hear me."

"Dude," Jeeter said, "don't you see how bad Sister Bessie is wanting to go in the house? You go in there with her—I'll keep my eye on the automobile."

While Dude was being urged to go into the house, Bessie went slowly across the porch to the door, waiting to see if Dude were following.

Ellie May drew herself up on her toes and tried to look into the bedroom through the open window. Ada was still busily engaged in straightening up the room, and

102

every few minutes she would push a chair across the floor and jerk an end of one of the beds into a new position.

"What is they going to do in there, Ma?" Ellie May asked.

Ada came to the window and leaned out. She pushed Ellie May's hands from the sill and motioned to her to go away.

"Sister Bessie and Dude is married," she said. "Now you go away and stop trying to see inside. You ain't got no business seeing of them."

After her mother had left the window, Ellie May again raised herself on the sill and looked inside.

Dude had gone as far as the front door, but he lingered there to take one more look at the automobile. He stood there until Ada came out and pushed him inside and made him go into the room with Bessie.

There was barely any furniture in the room. Besides the three double beds, there was a wobbly dresser in the corner, which was used as a washstand and a table. Over it, hanging on the wall was a cracked mirror. In the opposite end of the room was the fireplace. A broom-sedge sweeper stood behind the door, and another one, completely worn out, was under Ada's bed. There were also two straight-back chairs in the room. As there were no closets in the house, clothes were hanging on the walls by nails that had been driven into the two-by-four uprights.

The moment Dude walked into the room, Bessie slammed the door, and pulled him with her. She took the marriage license from her skirt pocket and held it in front of her.

"You hold one end, Dude, and I'll hold the other."

"What you going to do?"

"Marry us, Dude," she said.

"Didn't you get that all done at the courthouse in Fuller?"

"That wasn't all. I'm doing the balance now."

103

"When is we going to take a ride?" he asked.

"It won't be so very long now. We want to stay here a little while first. We got plenty of time to ride around, Dude."

"You going to let me drive it all the time?"

"Sure, you can drive it all the time. I don't know how to drive it, noway."

"You ain't going to let nobody else drive it, is you?"

"You is the only one who can drive it, Dude," she said. "But we got to hurry and finish marrying. You hold your end of the license while I pray."

Dude stood beside her, waiting for the prayer to be finished. She prayed silently for several minutes while he stood in front of her.

"I marry us man and wife. So be it. That's all, God. Amen."

There was a long silence while they looked at each other.

"When is we going for a ride?" Dude said.

"We is married now, Dude. We is finished being married. Ain't you glad of it?"

"When is we going for a ride?"

"I got to pray now," she said. "You kneel down on the floor while I make a little prayer."

They knelt down to pray. Dude got down on all fours, looking straight into Bessie's nose while her eyes were closed.

"Dear God, Dude and me is married now. We is wife and husband. Dude, he is an innocent young boy, unused to the sinful ways of the country, and I am a woman preacher of the gospel. You ought to make Dude a preacher, too, and let us use our new automobile in taking trips all over the country to pray for sinners. You ought to learn him how to be a fine preacher so we can make all the goats into sheep. That's all this time. We're

104

in a hurry now. Save us from the devil and make a place for us in heaven. Amen."

There was a rustle of skirts as Sister Bessie jumped to her feet and began running excitedly around the room. She came back and pulled at Dude, making him put his arms around her waist.

Outside in the yard, Jeeter and Ellie May had been standing on their toes looking in through the window to see what Dude and Bessie were doing. There were no curtains over the windows, and the board blinds had had to be opened so there would be light in the room.

Dude stood for several minutes watching Bessie as she tried to pull him across the room. She finally sat down on one of the beds and attempted to make him sit beside her.

"You ain't going to sleep now, is you?" he asked her. "It ain't time to go to bed yet. It ain't no more that noon-time now."

"Just for now," she said. "We can go out again after a while and take a ride in the automobile."

Dude ran to the window to look at the car. For the moment, he had completely forgotten about it. When he reached the window, he saw Jeeter and Ellie May holding to the sill with the ends of their fingers and trying to see inside.

"What you doing that for?" he asked Jeeter. "What you want to look at?"

Jeeter turned away and looked out over the brown broom-sedge. Ellie May ran around to the back of the house and tip-toed into the hall through the kitchen.

Bessie came to the window and pulled Dude around until he faced her. Then she made him go back and sit down on the bed.

Suddenly, without knowing how it happened, Dude found himself on the bed with a quilt over him. Bessie had locked her arms around him so tightly that he could not move in any direction.

Outside, he heard a ladder scrape against the weather-boards. Jeeter had found the ladder under the crib and had brought it to the window.

CHAPTER XII

WHEN Dude looked up, he saw that the door had been opened and that Ellie May, Ada, and the grandmother were crowding through it. He did not know what to do, but he tried to motion to them to go away.

He could not see Jeeter, because Jeeter was behind him, standing half-way up in the window with his feet supported on one of the rungs of the ladder. Bessie saw Jeeter, but she could not see the others.

Dude heard his grandmother groan and walk away. He could hear her feet sliding over the pine boards of the hall floor, the horse-collar shoes making an irritating sound as she went towards the front yard. He paid no more attention to the others.

After a while Jeeter cleared his throat and called Bessie. She did not answer him the first time he called, nor the next. Neither she nor Dude wanted to be disturbed.

When she persisted in not answering him, Jeeter climbed through the window and walked across the room to the bed. He shook Dude by the collar until he turned around.

Jeeter, however, did not have anything to say to Dude. It was Bessie he wanted to speak to.

"I been thinking just now about it, Sister Bessie, and the more I think it over in my mind, the more I convince myself that you was right about what we was discussing yesterday on the porch."

"What you want with me, Jeeter?" she asked.

"Now, about that place in the Bible where it says if a man's eye offends God he ought to go and take it out."

"That's what the Bible says," she answered.

"I know it does. And that's what's worrying my soul so bad right now."

"But you is a religious man, Jeeter," she said. "Nothing ought to bother your conscience now. I prayed for you about them turnips you took from Lov. The Lord has forgot all about it now. He ain't going to hound you none on that account."

"It ain't about the turnips. It's about cutting myself off. Now, I reckon what you said was right. I ought to go and do it."

Dude turned around and tried to push Jeeter to the floor. Jeeter clung to the bedstead, and would not move away.

"Why you want to do that?" Bessie said.

"I been thinking about all you said so much that right now I know I ought to go ahead and cut myself off, so the Lord won't let me be tempted no more. I offended Him, and I know I ought to cut myself off so I won't do it no more. Ain't that right, Sister Bessie?"

"That's right," she said. "That's what the Bible says a man ought to do when he's powerful sinful."

Jeeter looked at Bessie. He pulled back the quilt so he could see her better.

"Maybe I can put it off a little while, though," he said, after thinking several minutes. "Now, maybe it ain't so bad as I thought it was. This time of year puts a queer feeling into a man, and he says a lot of things he don't stop to take into account. Along about when the time to plow the land and put seed in the rows comes around, a

man feels like he ain't got no control over his tongue—
and don't want none. It's the same way with his actions.
I feel that way every late February and early March. No
matter how many children a man's got, he always wants
to get more."

There was a silence in the house for a long time. Ellie
May and Ada made no sound in the doorway. Jeeter sat
on the bed deep in thought until Dude pushed him to his
feet. Dude climbed out behind him.

When all of them were out in the yard again, Dude sat
in the automobile and blew the horn. The women were
busy wiping off the dust that had settled on the hood and
fenders. The grandmother, though, did not come close to
the car. She took her place behind a chinaberry tree and
watched every movement of the others.

Jeeter sat on his heels beside the chimney, and thought
over what Sister Bessie had said in the house. He was
more convinced than ever that God expected him to fix
himself so he would not have any more sinful thoughts
about Bessie.

He decided, however, not to carry out his intentions
just then. There was plenty of time left yet, he told himself, when he could go ahead and cut himself off, and so
long as he did it before he offended God any more, it
would be satisfactory. In the meanwhile, he would have
time in which to try to convince himself more thoroughly
that he should do it.

There was a little fat-back on rinds left in the kitchen,
and Ada had baked some cornbread. The bread had been
made with meal, salt, water, and grease.

All of them sat down at the table in the kitchen and ate
the fat-back and cornbread with full appetite. It was the
first time that day that any of them had had food, and it
would probably be the last. After the meat plate had been
wiped clean of grease, and after the last of the cornbread
was eaten, they went out into the yard again to look at

the new automobile. The grandmother had hidden a piece of the bread in her apron pocket, and she put it under the mattress of her bed so she would have something to eat the next day in case Jeeter failed to buy some more meal and meat.

Jeeter wanted to take a ride right away. He told Bessie he wanted to go, and that he was ready.

Bessie had other plans, however. She said she and Dude were going to take a little ride that afternoon all alone, so they could talk over their marriage together without any disturbance. She promised Jeeter she would let him ride when they came back.

She and Dude got in, and Dude drove the car out of the yard and into the tobacco road towards the State highway. Jeeter thought they might be going to Augusta, but before he could ask them if they were, they had gone too far to hear him call.

"That Dude is the luckiest man alive," he told Ellie May. "Now ain't he?"

Ellie May started down the road through the cloud of dust to see them leave. She heard Jeeter talking to her, but she was too much interested in seeing the new car go down the road and in hearing Dude blow the horn to listen to what Jeeter said.

"Dude, he has got a brand-new car to ride around in, and he's got married all at the same time," Jeeter continued. "There's not many men who get all that in the same day, I tell you. The new car is a fine piece of goods to own. There ain't nobody else that I know of between here and the river who has got a brand-new automobile. And there ain't many men who has a wife as fine-looking as Sister Bessie is at her age, neither. Bessie makes a fine woman for a man—any man, I don't care where you find him. She might be just a little bit more than Dude can take care of though, I fear. It looked to me like she requires a heap of satisfaction, one way and another, for a little woman no bigger than a gal. I don't know if Dude is that kind or not, but it won't take long for Bessie to find out. Now, if it was me, there wouldn't be no question of it. I'd please Sister Bessie coming and going, right from the start, and keep it up clear to the end."

Now Ellie May heard what Jeeter was saying, and it interested her. She waited to hear more.

"Now, you, Ellie May, it's time you was finding yourself a man. All my other children has got married. It's your time next. It was your time a long while ago, 'way before Pearl and Dude got married, but I make allowances for you on account of your face. I know it's harder for you to mate up than it is for anybody else, but in this country everybody has got to get mated up. You ought to go out and find yourself a man to marry right away, and not wait no longer. It might be too late pretty soon, and you don't want that to happen. It ain't going to get you nowhere fooling around with Lov like you was doing, because you can't get him that way. He's already married. It's the unmarried men you has got to get. There's a fine lot of boys running that sawmill over at Big Creek. You can walk over that way some day and make them take notice of you. It ain't hard to do. Women know how to make men take notice of them, and you're old enough to know all about it at your age. Them boys at the sawmill down there at Big Creek ought to take a liking to you in spite of the way you look in the face. When a man looks at you from behind, he ought to want to mate up with you right there and then. That's what I heard Lov say one time, and he ought to know, because he's mated up now. Just don't show your face too much, and that won't stop the boys from getting after you."

When Jeeter looked at Ellie May again, she was crying. It was about the first time he had ever seen her cry since she was a baby. He did not know what to do about it, nor to say about it, because he had never before had the occasion to try to calm a crying woman. Ada never cried. She never did anything.

Before he could ask her what the matter was, she had run off into the old cotton field; she ran towards the woods behind the house, jumping through the brown broom-sedge like a frightened rabbit.

"Now I never seen the likes of that before," Jeeter said, "I wonder what it was that I could have said that made her carry-on like that?"

CHAPTER XIII

JEETER remained seated on his heels by the chimney in the yard for half an hour after Ellie May had run away crying. He stared at the tracks left in the yard by the new automobile, amazed at the sharpness of the imprint of the tiretread. The tires of his own car, which was still standing in the yard between the house and the corn-crib, were worn smooth. When they rolled on the sand, they left no track, except two parallel bands of smoothed sand. He was wondering now what he could do about his tires. If he could pump them all up at the same time, he could haul a load of wood to Augusta and sell it. He might even get as much as a dollar for the load.

It was fifteen miles to the city, and after he had bought enough gasoline and oil for the trip there and back, there would not be much left of the dollar. A quarter, possibly, with which he could buy two or three jars of snuff and a peck of cotton-seed meal. Even a quarter would not buy enough corn meal for them to eat. He had already begun buying cotton-seed meal, because corn meal cost too much. Fifteen cents would buy enough cotton-seed meal to last them a whole week.

But Jeeter was not certain whether it was worth the trouble of hauling a load of wood. It would take him nearly half a day to load the car with blackjack, and half a day for the trip to Augusta. And then after he got there he might not be able to find anybody to buy it.

He still planned a crop for that year, though. He had by no means given up his plans to raise one. Ten or fifteen acres of cotton could be raised, if he could get the seed and guano. There was a mule over near Fuller he thought he could borrow, and he had a plow that would do; but it took money or an equal amount of credit to buy seed-cotton and guano. The merchants in Fuller had said they would not let him have anything on credit again, and it was useless to try to raise a loan in a bank in Augusta. He had tried to do that three or four times already, but the first thing they asked him was whom did he have to sign his notes, and what collateral had he to put up. Right there was where the deal fell through every time. Nobody would sign his notes, and he had nothing to put up for security. The men in the bank had told Jeeter to try a loan company.

The loan companies were the sharpest people he had ever had anything to do with. Once he had secured a two-hundred-dollar loan from one of them, but he swore it was the last time he would ever bind himself to such an agreement. To begin with, they came out to see him two or three times a week; some of them from the company's office would come out to the farm and try to tell him how to plant the cotton and how much guano to put in to the acre. Then on the first day of every month they came back to collect interest on the loan. He could never pay it, and they added the interest to the principal, and charged him interest on that, too.

By the time he sold his cotton in the fall, there was only seven dollars coming to him. The interest on the loan amounted to three per cent a month to start with, and at the end of ten months he had been charged thirty per cent, and on top of that another thirty per cent on the unpaid interest. Then to make sure that the loan was fully protected, Jeeter had to pay the sum of fifty dollars. He could never understand why he had to pay that, and the company did not undertake to explain it to him. When he had asked what the fifty dollars was meant to cover, he was told that it was merely the fee for making the loan. When the final settlement was made, Jeeter found that he had paid out more than three hundred dollars, and was receiving seven dollars for his share. Seven dollars for a year's labor did not seem to him a fair portion of the proceeds from the cotton, especially as he had done all the work, and had furnished the land and mule, too. He was even then still in debt, because he owed ten dollars for the hire of the mule he had used to raise the cotton. With Lov and Ada's help, he discovered that he had actually lost three dollars. The man who had rented him the mule insisted on being paid, and Jeeter had given him the seven dollars, and he was still trying to get the other three to pay the balance.

Jeeter swore that he would never again have anything to do with the rich people in Augusta. They had hounded him nearly every day, trying to tell him how he should cultivate the cotton, and in the end they came out and took it all away from him, leaving him three dollars in debt. He had done all the work, furnished the mule and the land, and yet the loan company had taken all the money the cotton brought, and made him lose three dollars. He told everybody he saw after that, that God was not working in a deal such as that one was. He told the men who represented the finance company the same thing, too.

"You rich folks in Augusta is just bleeding us poor people to death. You don't work none, but you get all the money us farmers make. Here I is working all the year myself, Dude plowing, and Ada and Ellie May helping to chop the cotton in summer and pick it in the fall, and what do I get out of it? Not a durn thing, except a debt of three dollars. It ain't right, I tell you. God ain't working on your side. He won't stand for such cheating much longer, neither. He ain't so liking of you rich people as you think He is. God, He likes the poor."

The men collecting for the loan company listened to Jeeter talk, and when he had finished, they laughed at him and got in their new automobile and drove back to Augusta.

That was one reason why Jeeter was not certain he could raise a crop that year. But he thought now that if he could get the seed and guano on credit from a man in Fuller, he would not be robbed. The people in Fuller were farmers, just as he was, or as he tried to be, and he did not believe they would cheat him. But every time he had said something about raising credit in Fuller, the merchants had waved him away and would not even listen to him.

"Ain't no use in talking no more, Jeeter," they had said. "There's farmers coming into Fuller every day from all over the country wanting the same thing. If there's one, there's a hundred been here. But we can't help you people none. Last year we let some of you farmers have seed-cotton and guano on credit, and when fall came there was durn little cotton made, and what there was didn't bring more than seven cents, middling grade. Ain't no sense in farming when things is like that. And we can't take no more chances. All of us has just got to wait until the rich give up the money they're holding back."

"But, praise God, me and my folks is starving out there on that tobacco road. We ain't got nothing to eat, and we ain't got nothing to sell that will bring money to get meal and meat. You storekeepers won't let us have no more credit since Captain John left, and what is we going to do? I don't know what's going to happen to me and my folks if the rich don't stop bleeding us. They've got all the money, holding it in the banks, and they won't lend it out

116

unless a man will cut off his arms and leave them there for security."

"The best thing you can do, Jeeter," they had said, "is to move your family up to Augusta, or across the river in South Carolina to Horsecreek Valley, where all the mills is, and go to work in one of them. That's the only thing left for you to do now. Ain't no other way."

"No! By God and by Jesus, no!" Jeeter had said. "That's one thing I ain't going to do! The Lord made the land, and He put me here to raise crops on it. I been doing that, and my daddy before me, for the past fifty years, and that's what's intended. Them durn cotton mills is for the women folks to work in. They ain't no place for a man to be, fooling away with little wheels and strings all day long. I say, it's a hell of a job for a man to spend his time winding strings on spools. No! We was put here on the land where cotton will grow, and it's my place to make it grow. I wouldn't fool with the mills if I could make as much as fifteen dollars a week in them. I'm staying on the land till my time comes to die."

"Have it your own way, Jeeter, but you'd better think it over and go to work in the cotton mills. That's what nearly everybody else around Fuller has done. Some of them is in Augusta and some of them is in Horsecreek Valley, but they're all working in the cotton mills just the same. You and your wife together could make twenty or twenty-five dollars a week doing that. You ain't making nothing by staying here. You'll both have to go and live at the county poor-farm pretty soon if you stay here and try to raise cotton."

"Then it will be the rich who put us there," Jeeter had said. "If we has to go to the poor-farm and live, it will be because the rich has got all the money that ought to be spread out among us all and won't turn it loose and give me some credit to get seed-cotton and guano with."

"You ain't got a bit of sense, Jeeter. You ought to know

117

by now that you can't farm. It takes a rich man to run a farm these days. The poor has got to work in the mills."

"Maybe I ain't got much sense, but I know it ain't intended for me to work in the mills. The land was where I was put at the start, and it's where I'm going to be at the end."

"Why, even your children has got more sense than you, Jeeter. They didn't stay here to starve. They went to work in the mills. Now, there's Lizzie Belle up there in — ——"

"Maybe some of them did, but that ain't saying it was right. Dude, he didn't go, noway. He's still here. He's going to farm the land some day, just like all of us ought to be doing."

"Dude hasn't got the sense to leave. If he had the sense your other children had, he wouldn't stay here. He would be able to see how foolish it is to try to farm like things is now. The rich ain't aiming to turn loose their money for credit. They're going to hold on to it all the time to run the mills with."

Jeeter remembered all that had been said, as he sat on his heels by the chimney, leaning against the warm bricks in the late February sun. He had heard men in Fuller say things like that dozens of times, and it always had ended in his walking out and leaving them. None of them understood how he felt about the land when the plowing season came each spring.

The feeling was in him again. This time he felt it more deeply than ever, because in all the past six or seven years when he had wanted to raise a crop he had kept his disappointment from crushing his spirit by looking forward to the year when he could farm again. But this year he felt that if he did not get the seed-cotton and guano in the ground he would never be able to try again. He knew he could not go on forever waiting each year for credit and never receiving it, because he was becoming weaker each day, and soon he would not be able to walk between the plow-handles even if credit were provided for him.

It was because of his discouragement that the odor of wood and sedge smoke and of newly turned earth now filling the air, was so strong and pungent. Farmers everywhere were burning over the woods and the broom-sedge fields, and plowing the earth in the old cotton lands and in the new grounds.

The urge he felt to stir the ground and to plant cotton in it, and after that to sit in the shade during the hot months watching the plants sprout and grow, was even greater than the pains of hunger in his stomach. He could sit calmly and bear the feeling of hunger, but to be compelled to live and look each day at the unplowed fields was an agony he believed he could not stand many more days.

His head dropped forward on his knees, and sleep soon overcame him and brought a peaceful rest to his tired heart and body.

CHAPTER XIV

DUDE and Sister Bessie came back at sunset. Dude was blowing the horn a mile away, when Jeeter first heard it, and he and Ada ran out to the road to watch them come. The horn made a pretty sound, Jeeter thought, and he liked the way Dude blew it. He was pressing the horn button and taking his finger off every few seconds, like the firemen who blew the engine whistles when they were leaving the coal chute.

"That's Dude blowing the horn," Jeeter said. "Don't he blow it pretty, though? He always liked to blow the horn near about as much as he liked to drive an automobile. He used to cuss a lot because the horn on my car wouldn't make the least bit of a sound. The wires got pulled loose and I never had time to tie them up again."

Ada stood in the road watching the shiny new car come nearer and nearer. It looked like a big black chariot, she said, running away from a cyclone. The dust blown up behind did look like the approach of a cyclone.

"Ain't that the *prettiest* sight to see?" she said.

"That's Dude driving it, and blowing the horn, too," he said. "It makes a pretty sound when it blows, don't it, Ada?"

Jeeter was proud of his son.

"I wish all my children was here to see it," Ada said.

"Lizzie Belle used to like to look at automobiles, and ride in them, too, more than anybody I ever saw. Maybe she's got herself one now. I wish I knowed."

Sister Bessie and Dude drove up slowly, and turned into the yard. Jeeter and Ada ran along beside the car until it stopped beside the chimney of the house. Ellie May saw everything from around the corner of the house.

"How far a piece did you go riding?" Jeeter asked Bessie as she opened the door and stepped out on the ground. "You been gone clear the whole afternoon. Did you go to Augusta?"

Bessie caught up the bottom of her skirt and began wiping off the dust. Ada and Ellie May were already at work on the other side of the car. The grandmother was thirty feet away, standing behind a chinaberry tree and looking around the trunk at the automobile. Dude sat under the steering-wheel blowing the horn.

"We went and we went till we went clear to McCoy," she said. "We just kept on going till we got there."

"That's about thirty miles, ain't it?" Jeeter asked excitedly. "Did you go clear that far and back?"

"That's what we did," Dude said. "I ain't never been that far away from here before. It's a pretty country down that way, too."

"Why didn't you go to Augusta?" Jeeter asked. "You went down to the crossroads and I thought sure you was going to Augusta."

"We didn't go that way," Dude said, "we went the other way—toward McCoy. And we went clear to McCoy, too."

Jeeter walked to the front of the car and looked at it. Dude climbed out and stopped blowing the horn for a while.

"Praise the Lord," Jeeter said, "what went and done that?"

He pointed to the right front fender and headlight.

Everybody stopped dusting and gathered around the radiator. The fender was twisted and crumpled until it looked as if somebody had taken a sledge-hammer and tried to see how completely he could maul it. The right headlight had been knocked off. Only a piece of twisted iron and a small strand of insulated wire remained where it had been. The fender had been mashed back against the hood.

"It was a wagon what done that," Dude said. "We was coming back from McCoy, and I was looking out at a big turpentine still, and then the first thing I knowed we was smashed smack into the back end of a two-horse wagon."

Bessie looked at the mashed fender and missing headlight, but she said nothing. She could hardly blame it on the devil this time, as she had been riding in the car herself when the accident occurred, but it seemed to her that God ought to have taken better care of it, especially after she had stopped and prayed about it when she bought the automobile that morning in Fuller.

"It don't hurt the running of it none, though, does it?" Jeeter asked.

"It runs like it was brand new yet," Dude said. "And the horn wasn't hurt none at all. It blows just as pretty as it did this morning."

The fender had been crumpled beyond repair. It was lying against the hood of the car and, except for the jagged edges, it appeared as if it had been removed. Apparently nothing else, with the exception of the headlight, had been damaged; there were no dents in the body, and the wheels and axle seemed to stand straight and in line. The broken spring made the left rear end sag, however.

"That don't hurt it none," Jeeter said. Don't pay no attention to it, Bessie. Just leave it be, and you'll never know it was any different then it was when you got it brand new."

"That's right," she said. "I ain't letting it worry me none, because it wasn't Dude's fault. He was looking at the big turpentine still alongside the road, and I was too, when the wagon got in our way. The nigger driving it ought to have had enough sense to get out of our way when he heard us coming."

"Wasn't you blowing the horn then, Dude?" Jeeter said.

"Not right then I wasn't, because I was busy looking at the big still. I never saw one that big nowhere before. It was almost as big as a corn-liquor still, only it wasn't as shiny-looking."

"It's a shame to get the new car smashed up so soon already, though," Bessie said, going back and wiping off the dust. "It was brand new only a short time before noon, and now it's only sundown."

"It was that nigger," Dude said. "If he hadn't been asleep on the wagon it wouldn't have happened at all. He was plumb asleep till it woke him up and threw him out in the ditch."

"He didn't get hurt much, did he?" Jeeter asked.

"I don't know about that," Dude said. "When we drove off again, he was still lying in the ditch. The wagon turned over on him and mashed him. His eyes was wide open all the time, but I couldn't make him say nothing. He looked like he was dead."

"Niggers will get killed. Looks like there ain't no way to stop it."

The sun had been down nearly half an hour and the chill dampness of an early spring night settled over the ground. The grandmother had already gone into the house and got into bed. Ada went up on the porch, hugging her arms across her chest to keep warm, and Bessie started inside, too.

Dude and Jeeter stood around the car until it was so dark they could not see it any longer, and then they too went inside.

123

The glare of woods-fire soon began to light the sky on the horizons, and the smell of pine smoke filled the damp evening air. Fires were burning in all directions; some of them had been burning a week or longer, while others had been burning only since that afternoon.

In the spring, the farmers burned over all of their land. They said the fire would kill the boll-weevils. That was the reason they gave for burning the woods and fields, whenever anybody asked why they did not stop burning up young pine seedlings and standing timber. But the real reason was because everybody had always burned the woods and fields each spring, and they saw no cause for abandoning life-long habits. Burning fields and woods seemed to them to be as necessary as drilling guano in the cotton fields to make the plants yield a large crop. If the wood that was burned had been sawn into lumber or cut into firewood, instead of burning to ashes on the ground, there would have been something for them to sell. Boll-weevils were never killed in any great numbers by the fire; the cotton plants had to be sprayed with poison in the summer, anyway. But everybody had always burned over the land each spring, and they continued if only for the reason that their fathers had done it. Jeeter always burned over his land, even though there was no reason in the world why he should do it; he never raised crops any more. This was why the land was bare of everything except broom-sedge and blackjack; the sedge grew anew each year, and the hottest fire could not hurt those tough scrub oaks.

Inside the house the women gathered in the bedroom in the darkness and waited for Jeeter and Dude. The grandmother was already in bed, covered with her ragged quilts. Ellie May had gone out into the broom-sedge and had not yet returned. Bessie and Ada sat on the beds waiting.

The three beds had always held all the Lesters, even

124

when there were sometimes as many as eight or nine of them there. Occasionally, some had slept on pallets on the floor in summer, but in winter it was much warmer for every one in the beds. Now that all of the children had left except Dude and Ellie May, there was just enough room for every one. Bessie had a house of her own, a three-room tenant house on the last sand hill at the river; but the roof was rotten, and the shingles had blown away, and when it rained everything in the three rooms was soaked with water.

Sometimes in the middle of the night when a storm came up suddenly, Bessie would wake up to find the bed filled with water, every piece of her clothes wet, and more water pouring down through the roof. She had told Ada that she did not want to stay there any more until she could have a new shingle roof put on the house. The building and the land around it belonged to Captain John Harmon; he never came out to the tobacco road any more, and he made no repairs to the buildings. He had told Jeeter and Bessie, and all the other people who lived out there, that they could stay in the houses until the buildings rotted to the ground and that he would never ask for a penny of rent. They understood the arrangement fully; he was not going to make any repairs to the roofs, porches, rotted under-sills, or anything about the buildings. If the houses fell down, he said, it would be too bad for them; but if they stood up, then Jeeter, Bessie, and all the others could remain in them as long as they wanted to stay.

Jeeter and Dude came into the house, stumbling through the darkness. There was a lamp in the house, but no kerosene had been bought that whole winter. The Lesters went to bed at dark, except in summer when it was warm enough to sit on the porch, and they got up at daylight. There was no need for kerosene, anyway.

Jeeter sat down on his bed beside Ada and pulled off

125

his heavy shoes. The brogans fell on the floor like bricks dropped waist high.

"We stopped in every house we came to, and got out and visited a while," Bessie said. "Some of them wanted prayer, and some didn't. It didn't make much difference to me, because me and Dude was all excited about riding around. Some of the people wanted to know where I got all the money to buy a brand-new car, and why I married Dude, and I told them. I told them my former husband left me eight hundred dollars, and I said I married Dude because I was going to make a preacher out of him. Of course, that was only one reason why we got married, but I knew that would be enough to tell them."

"Nobody said things against you, did they, Sister Bessie?" Jeeter asked. "Some people has got a way of talking about people like us."

"Well, some of them did say a few things about me marrying Dude. They said he was too young to be married to a woman my age, but when they started talking like that, we just got in our new automobile and rode off. A lot of them said it was a sin and a shame for to take my husband's money and buy an automobile and get married to a young boy like Dude, but while they was doing the talking, me and Dude was doing the riding, wasn't we, Dude?"

Dude did not answer.

"I reckon Dude has gone to sleep," Jeeter said. "He worked pretty hard to-day, driving that automobile clear to McCoy and back again."

Ada sat up in bed.

"Take them overalls off, Jeeter," she said angrily. "I ain't never seen the like of it. You know I ain't going to let you sleep in the bed with them dirty pants on. I have to tell you about it nearly every time. They dirty-up the bed something bad. You ought to know I ain't going to stand for that."

"It's pretty cold again to-night," Jeeter said. "I get chilly when I don't sleep with my overalls on. It seems like I can't do nothing no more like I want to. Sleeping in overalls ain't going to hurt nothing, noway."

"You're the only man I ever knowed of who wanted to sleep in his overalls. Don't nobody else do like that."

Jeeter did not answer her. He got up out of bed and climbed out of his overalls and hung them on the foot of the bed. When he got back under the quilts, he was shivering all over.

Bessie could be heard over on the other side of the room stepping around in her stockinged feet getting ready for bed. She had kept her shoes on until she removed her clothes.

Jeeter lifted his head from under the cover and tried to look through the darkness of the room.

"You know, Bessie," he said, "it sort of makes me feel good like I was before I lost my health to have a woman preacher sleep in my house. It's a fine feeling I has about you staying here."

"I'm a woman preacher, all right," she said, "but I ain't no different in other ways from the rest of the women-folks. Jeeter, you know that, don't you?"

Jeeter raised himself on his elbow and strained his eyes to see through the darkness across the room.

"I hope you ain't leaving us no time soon," he said. "I'd be powerful pleased to have you sleep here all the time, Bessie."

Ada thrust her elbow into his ribs with all her strength, and he fell down groaning with pain on the bed beside her.

Bessie could be heard getting into her bed. The cornshuck mattress crackled, and the slats rattled as she lay down and stretched out her feet. She lay still for several minutes, and then she began to stretch her hands out towards the other side, the impact of her arms making the shucks crackle more than ever.

127

Suddenly she sat up in bed, throwing the quilts aside. "Where's Dude?" she demanded angrily, her voice gruff and unnatural. "Where is you, Dude?"

Not a sound was to be heard in the room. Ada had sat upright, and Jeeter had sprung to a sitting position on the side of the bed. Bessie's corn-shuck mattress crackled some more, and then the thump of her bare feet on the pine floor could be heard all over the house. Jeeter still did not attempt to speak or to move. He waited to catch every sound in the house.

"You Dude—you Dude!" Bessie cried from the centre of the room, trying to feel her way from bed to bed. "Where is you, Dude—why don't you answer me? You'd better not try to hide from me, Dude!"

"What's the matter, Bessie?" Jeeter said.

"Dude ain't in the bed—I can't find him nowhere at all."

Reaching for his overalls, Jeeter jumped to his feet. He began fumbling in his pockets for a match. At last he found one, and bending over, he struck it on the floor.

The flare of the match revealed every one in the room. Every one was there except Ellie May and Dude. Bessie was only a few feet away from Jeeter, and he tried to look at her. She was shielding her eyes from the light.

Ada crawled out of bed and stood behind Jeeter the moment she saw Bessie.

"Put them overalls on," she commanded Jeeter. "I don't know what you and her is up to, but I'm watching. You put them overalls on right now. I don't care if she is a woman preacher, she ain't got no right to stand in the floor in front of you like she is."

Jeeter hesitated, and the match burned down to his fingers. He stepped into his overalls, put one arm through a gallus, and reached into his pocket for another match.

Bessie was still standing beside Jeeter, but when he struck the match, she ran to Mother Lester's bed. She

128

jerked back the covers, and saw Dude sound asleep. The grandmother was awake, and she lay trembling in her old torn black clothes.

Jeeter shook Dude awake and pulled him to the floor. Ada jerked him by the arm.

"What you mean by not getting in bed with Bessie?" Jeeter demanded, shaking him roughly by the collar.

Dude looked around him and blinked his eyes. He was unable to see anything in the flare of the match.

"What you want?" he asked, rubbing his eyes.

"Dude, he didn't know which bed to get in," Sister Bessie said tenderly. "He was so tired and sleepy he didn't look to see which one we was going to sleep in, did you, Dude?"

"Dude, you can't act that way," Jeeter said. "You got to keep your eyes open when you get married. Bessie, here, got powerful nervous when she didn't find you in bed."

Ada went back to bed, and Jeeter followed her. He did not take off his overalls, and Ada went to sleep without thinking about them.

Ellie May came in after a while and got into bed with her grandmother. No one spoke to her.

The grandmother had been wide awake all the time, but no one said anything to her, and she did not try to tell Bessie that Dude was in her bed. No one ever said anything to her, except to tell her to get out of the way, or to stop eating the bread and meat.

Dude and Bessie went to their bed and lay down. Sister Bessie tried to talk to Dude, but Dude was tired and sleepy. He did not answer her. The rustling sound of the corn-shuck mattress continued most of the night.

CHAPTER XV

Jeeter drank his third cup of chicory and cleared his throat. Dude had already left the kitchen and gone to the yard, and Sister Bessie was on the back porch combing her hair. Jeeter went down the back steps and leaned against the well.

"It would be a pretty smart deal if I was to take a load of wood to Augusta to-day," he said. "Me and Dude's got a big pile of it all cut and ready to haul. Now, if we was to pile it in the new automobile it wouldn't take no time to haul it to the city, would it, Bessie?"

She finished combing her hair, stuck half a dozen pins and the rhinestone comb into it, and walked with Jeeter over to the automobile.

"Maybe it would hold a load," she said. "There ain't so much room in the back seat, though."

"Mine holds a fair load, and it ain't no bigger than that one. They is the same kind of automobiles. The only difference being that yours is near about a brand-new one now."

Dude turned on the switch and raced the engine. The motor hummed perfectly. The tightness that had bothered Dude the day before had gone, and the engine was in good running order. He blew the horn several times, grinning at Jeeter.

"I'd sort of like to take a trip to Augusta, all right,"

Bessie said. "Me and Dude was going there yesterday, before we changed our mind and went down to McCoy instead."

"It won't take long to put a load of wood in the back seat," Jeeter said. "We can leave pretty soon. Dude—you drive the automobile out across the field yonder to that pile of wood we been cutting the past week. I'll get some pieces of baling wire to bind the load good and tight so it won't drop off."

Bessie got in beside Dude, and they started out across the old cotton field towards the grove of blackjack. The field had grown up into four-foot broom-sedge in the past few years. Once it had been the finest piece of tobacco land on the whole farm.

The rows of the last crop of cotton were still there, and as the car gathered speed, the bumps tossed Dude and Bessie up and down so suddenly and so often that they could not keep their seats. Dude grasped the steering-wheel tightly and held himself better than Bessie could; Bessie bobbed up and down as the car raced over the old cotton rows and her head hit the top every time there was a bump. They had gone about a quarter of a mile, and were almost at the edge of the grove where the pile of blackjack was, when suddenly there was a jarring crash that stopped the car dead in its tracks.

Dude was thrown against the steering-wheel, and Bessie shot forward off the seat and struck her head against the wind-shield. Where her forehead had hit the glass there were a hundred or more cracks, branching out like a wet spider-web in the sunshine. None of the glass shattered, though, and the wind-shield was still intact. She did not know what had happened.

"Praise the Lord," Bessie shouted, pulling herself out of her cramped position on the floor-boards. "What's we done this time, Dude?"

"I reckon we rammed into a stump," he said. "I clear

forgot about them old dead stumps out here in the sedge. I couldn't see nothing at all for the sedge. It covers everything on the ground."

Both of them got out and went to the front. A two-foot stump had stopped them.

The blackened pine stump, hidden from view by the four-foot wall of brown broom-sedge, stood squarely in front of the axle. It was partly decayed, and except for the heart of it, the car would have knocked it down and gone ahead without any trouble. As it was, the axle was not badly bent; actually the car was going only fifteen miles an hour, and there had not been enough force to twist the axle out of shape. The wheels had sprung forward a few inches, but aside from that, there was nothing to worry about. The car was still almost as good as new.

Jeeter came running up just then with his hands and arms full of rusty baling wire, which he had found behind the corn-crib.

They did not have to tell him what had happened, because he could see just as well as they did that the front axle had hit the stump and sprung the wheels forward several inches.

"It don't appear to be hurt much," he said. "Maybe it ain't hurt none at all. We has got to haul a load of wood to Augusta to-day, because there ain't no more meal and chicory in the house to eat."

Bessie watched Dude start up the engine and back away from the stump. He swung around it, and drove carefully the remaining few yards to the pile of blackjack. Jeeter began picking up the pieces of scrub oak and hurling them like javelins into the back seat.

"I reckon I'd better put the top down," Dude said. "It won't hold much unless the top's down."

He began unfastening the set screws holding the top to the wind-shield, while Jeeter and Bessie continued to hurl blackjack into the back seat.

132

"There won't be no room for Ada to go along, too, will there?" Jeeter said. "She'll be powerful put out when she sees us drive off to Augusta and not stopping to take her along. The last time me and Dude went up there in my car, she and Ellie May liked to had a fit, but it wasn't no use, because we needed all the room for wood."

"Well, I ain't going to stay at home," Bessie said. "I'm going just as big as the next one. You can't make me stay here."

"I'm going," Dude said. "Can't nobody make me stay here. I'm going to drive the car."

He had thrown the top back and was trying to tie it down. Most of it had been folded up, but some of it hung down as far as the rear axle. He could not find any means of making it stay folded, so he allowed it to hang down behind.

"I sure ain't going to miss going," Jeeter said. "It's my wood I'm taking to sell. I'm going to be the first one to go."

The scrub oak had been cut into varying lengths the past week when Jeeter and Dude had spent a day in the grove getting a load ready to sell. Some of it was a foot in length, but most of it was anywhere from three to six feet long. The length in which it had been cut was the length of the stunted trees after they had been hacked off with an axe at the stump. As soon as a tree was hacked down, Jeeter had taken the axe and broken the limbs off, and then the wood was ready to haul. The blackjack never grew much taller than a man's head; it was a stunted variety of oak that used its sap in toughening the fibres instead of growing new layers and expanding the old, as other trees did. The blackjack sticks were about two or three inches in diameter, and wiry and tough as heavy pieces of wire or small iron water-pipes.

It took them about half an hour to pile on as much wood as the back seat would hold. After that, Jeeter began binding it to the body with baling wire so none of it would drop off along the road while they were riding to Augusta. The ends of the blackjack protruded in all directions, sticking out several feet on each side and behind. Others had been jabbed straight into the upholstery, and they appeared to be the only ones that did not need fastening. The rusty baling wire broke nearly every time Jeeter attempted to fasten it to the door-handles, and he would have to stop and splice the ends, twisting them until they would hold. The task of loading the blackjack and tying it on to the car took nearly two hours, and even then several pieces of wood fell off when one of them touched the car or leaned against it.

With the wood in place, Dude drove back across the field towards the house, going no faster than a man's walk, but even then the wood persisted in falling off. Jeeter and Bessie came behind, picking up the sticks and carrying them to the house.

Ada and Ellie May were in the yard when they got there. The grandmother waited behind a chinaberry tree to see what they were going to do. Ada stood squarely in front of the car, waiting to find out where she was going to sit. The grandmother went to the corner of the house and stood there, all except her face hidden from view.

"Where is I going to sit and ride?" Ada said. "I don't see no sitting place for nobody much, with all that wood you got loaded."

Jeeter waited several minutes, hoping that Bessie would undertake to answer Ada. When she did not, Jeeter got in and sat down beside Dude.

"There ain't no room for you," he said.

"Why ain't there no room for me, if there's room for you and Dude and that hussy, there?"

"Sister Bessie ain't no hussy," Jeeter said. "She ain't nothing like that. She's a woman preacher."

134

"Being a woman preacher don't keep her from being a hussy. That could help to make her a bigger one. Something acts that way, because she is a big old hussy."

"What make you say that about Bessie?" he said.

"Last night she was walking all around the room with none of her clothes on. If I hadn't made you put on your overalls when I did, there ain't no telling what she might have done. She's a hussy."

"Now, Ada," he said, "you ought not to talk like that about Bessie. She's a woman preacher, and she's married to Dude, too."

"That don't make no difference. She's a hussy, all the same. She always fools around with the men-folks. She don't never stay in the house and help clean it up like I has to do. She's taking after the men-folks because she's a hussy. When she goes preaching, she always does the preaching to the men-folks and don't pay no attention to the women-folks at all."

"I ain't got nothing to say against Sister Bessie. She's a woman preacher, and what she does is the Lord's doings. He instructs her what to do."

"Ada is peeved because I married Dude and came here to stay," Bessie said to Jeeter. "She don't like it because I'm going to stay in the room."

"You shut your mouth now, Ada," Jeeter said, "and let us be going. I got to sell this load of wood in Augusta to-day."

Dude started the car, and Bessie got in and sat on the edge of the seat beside Jeeter. There was barely enough room for all three of them.

Ada ran towards them, trying to jump on the running-board, but Dude speeded up the car and she could not get on. When he suddenly cut the wheels and turned out of the yard into the tobacco road, the rear wheel barely missed running over Ada's feet. She shouted after them, but the car was going so fast by that time that it was use-

135

less to run after them and try to stop them. She went back into the yard and, with Ellie May, stood looking at the cloud of dust that hid the car from view. The grandmother came from behind the corner of the house and, picking up the old croker sack, started to the thicket for dead twigs. She was already hungry again, although she had had a cup of chicory only two or three hours before.

Dude slowed down when they approached the crossroad where they were to turn off the tobacco road and enter the State highway to Augusta. He did not slow down enough, however, because the momentum swung the load of blackjack to the offside, and the entire top of the pile fell in the road.

Jeeter and Dude worked half an hour getting the wood in place again, and with Bessie helping the little that she could, it was then ready to be tied down again. Jeeter went across the field to a negro cabin and borrowed two plow-lines. He came back and threw them over the wood and tied the ends down tightly.

"Now, that will hold it, durn that blackjack," he said. "There ain't nothing else in the world like plow-lines and baling wire. The two together is the best in the world to do anything with. Give me a little of both and I can do any kind of job."

They were off again, speeding down the highway towards Augusta. The city was now only twelve miles away.

Dude was a good driver, all right; he swung out of the tracks just at the right moment every time he met another automobile. Only two or three times did he almost run head-on into other cars. He was so busy blowing the horn that he forgot to drive on the right-hand side of the road until the last minute. Most of the cars they met gave them plenty of road when they heard the horn blowing.

Jeeter could not talk, because he was holding his breath most of the time. The swiftness of the car frightened him so badly he could not answer Bessie's questions.

She looked grimly ahead most of the time, proud of her automobile and hoping that the negroes and farmers they passed in the fields beside the road would know it belonged to her instead of thinking it was Jeeter's or Dude's.

It was between noon and one o'clock when they reached the half-way point. Augusta was then only a little over seven miles away, and when they got to the top of the last hill they would be able to see the city down in the valley beside the big muddy river.

The last hill they had to climb before reaching that point was a long one. It was a mile and a half from the creek at the bottom to the filling-station on top, and they were about half way up, when suddenly the car slowed down to a few miles an hour. The water was boiling in the engine and radiator, and steam shot higher than the top of the wind-shield. The engine was making a great noise, too. It sounded as if it were knocking in the same way that Jeeter's old car had, only a little harder and a little louder.

"What's the matter with us?" Bessie said, leaning over the door and looking around outside.

"It must have got hot climbing the hill," Dude said. "I don't know what else is wrong with it."

They went a hundred yards, and the car stopped. The engine choked down, and the steam whistled out of the pipes like pistons on a freight train at the coal chute.

Jeeter jumped out and shoved a big rock under the rear wheel before Dude could put on the brakes. The car stopped rolling backwards.

"What's the matter with it, Dude?" Bessie said again. "Is something gone wrong?"

"I reckon it just got hot," he said.

He made no effort to get out. He sat under the steering-wheel, grasping it tightly and jerking it from side to side as far as it would go. Presently he began blowing the horn again.

"That won't help it none, Dude," Jeeter said. "You'll wear out that durn horn before you know it, if you keep doing that all the time. Why don't you get out and try to do something?"

Several automobiles passed them at high speed, going up the hill and coming down, but none of them slowed up or stopped to offer help.

Another car was coming slowly up the hill behind them. It was coming very slowly in low gear, and it was steaming like Bessie's new car. As it chugged slowly past them, some of the negroes leaned out and looked at the stalled automobile.

One of them called to Jeeter.

"What's the matter with your automobile, white-folks? It looks like it ain't going to run no more."

"By God and by Jesus!" Jeeter said, angrily. "What's your name, nigger? Where you from?"

"We come from Burke County," he said. "What you want to know that for, white-folks?"

Before Jeeter could say anything more, the negroes' car was a hundred yards up the hill, and gaining speed. Jeeter had been going to make them pull Bessie's car up the hill, if he could have stopped them.

Dude cranked up the engine and put the car into gear. Jeeter and Bessie hopped on the running-board just in time, because Dude soon had the car going fast. The engine had cooled, and they were going faster than the negroes' car. They gained on the car ahead and were getting ready to pass it, when suddenly the engine began knocking louder than ever, and they came to a stop.

"This is the durndest automobile I ever saw," Jeeter said. "It don't do the same thing long enough to make me accustomed."

They had stopped this time on top of the hill. Dude was getting ready to let it roll down, when Jeeter saw the filling-station, and he told Dude to wait a minute.

"I'll bring some water and put it in," he said.

He crossed the road and went into the filling-station. He was back in a few minutes carrying a bucket of water. The man who ran the station came out with him.

While Jeeter was unscrewing the radiator cap, the other man was raising the hood to measure the oil.

"The trouble with you people, brother," he said, "is you ain't got a drop of oil in your car. Your bearings is burned out. How far did you come from?"

Jeeter told him they lived near Fuller on the old tobacco road.

"You've already ruined your new car," he said. "That's a shame. I hate to see people who don't know no better ruining automobiles."

"What's wrong with it now?" Bessie said.

"Your new car is ruined, sister. It'll take a gallon and a half of oil to put enough in it to run on. Do you want me to fill it up for you?"

"How much does it cost?" Bessie said.

"A dollar and a half."

"I didn't aim to pay out money on it."

"Well, it won't run no more unless you put oil in it. It looks to me like you didn't have enough in it to start with."

"I ain't got but two dollars," she said. "I was going to buy gasoline with most of that."

"Me and Dude ain't got none," Jeeter said. "But when I sell this load of wood, I'll have a dollar and a half, maybe."

"You pour the oil into it," Bessie said. "I don't want to ruin my new automobile. I bought it brand new in Fuller yesterday."

"It's already ruint, sister," the man said, "but you'll have to put oil in it if you're going in to Augusta and back to Fuller again."

They waited while he poured the oil in, and then Bes-

139

sie gave him the money. She had the bills tied in a hand-kerchief, and it took her several minutes to untie the hard knots.

Dude started the engine, and they moved slowly off the hill-top and rolled down the long grade to Augusta. The car was running like new again by the time they reached the bottom of the hill, but the engine made more noise than the one in Jeeter's car. The bearings and connecting rods were so loose they made a jingling sound when the car was going more than fifteen miles an hour down hill.

CHAPTER XVI

THREE hours had already been spent in trying to sell the load of blackjack. Apparently there was not a man in Augusta who wanted to buy it. At some of the houses Jeeter went to, the people at first said they needed wood, but after they had asked him how much he wanted for it they were suspicious. Jeeter told them he was asking only a dollar, and then they asked him if he were selling split pine at that small price. He had to explain that it was blackjack, and not even sawn into stove length. The next thing he knew the door was slammed in his face, and he had to go to the next house and try again.

At a little after six o'clock the wood was still piled on the back seat of the car, and no buyer was in sight. Jeeter began stopping people on the streets in a final and desperate effort to dispose of the wood at fifty cents; but the men and women he approached took one look at the blackjack piled on the car and walked off, evidently thinking it was a joke of some kind. Nobody was foolish enough to buy blackjack when pine wood burned better and was less trouble to use.

"I don't know what we're going to do," Jeeter told Bessie. "It's getting almost too late to go back home, and nobody wants to buy wood no more. I used to sell it with no effort any time I brought a load up here."

Dude said he was hungry, and that he wanted to go somewhere and eat. Sister Bessie had half a dollar; Jeeter had nothing. Dude, of course, had nothing.

Jeeter had planned to sell the wood for a dollar, and then to buy some meat and meal to take home to eat; but he did not know what to do now. He turned to Bessie questioningly.

"Maybe we better start back toward Fuller," she said. "I can buy two gallons of gasoline, and that ought to be enough."

"Ain't we going to eat nothing?" Dude said. "My poor belly is as dry as the drought."

"Maybe we could sell something else," Jeeter said, looking at the automobile. "I don't know what we has got to sell, though."

"We ain't going to sell my new automobile," Bessie said quickly. "It was brand new only yesterday. That's one thing nobody ain't going to sell."

Jeeter looked the car over from front to back.

"No, I wouldn't think of doing nothing like that. But you know, Bessie, maybe we could sell a wee biddy piece of it, sort of."

He walked around the car and grasped the spare tire and wheel in his hands. He shook it violently.

"It's near about loose, anyhow," he said. "It wouldn't hurt the new car none, Bessie."

"Well, I reckon we got to," she said slowly. "That tire and wheel ain't doing us no good, noway. We can't ride on but four of them at a time, and five is a big waste."

They drove around the block until they found a garage. Jeeter went in and made inquiry. Presently a man came out, took the tire and wheel off, and rolled it through the garage door.

Jeeter came walking briskly across the street, holding out several green notes. He counted them one by one before Bessie and Dude.

"Ain't we lucky folks, though?" he said.

"How much money did it bring?" she asked.

"He said three dollars was more than enough, but that much sounded like a heap of money to me. And here it is! Ain't they pretty and new, though? Out there at Fuller all the money I ever saw was just about ready to fall apart, it was that worn out. Up here in Augusta the people has got good money."

The next stop was a small grocery store. Jeeter got out and bought a large sack of soda crackers and two pounds of yellow cheese. He came back to the car and offered the food to Dude and Bessie. They all broke off chunks of cheese and stuffed their mouths full of crackers.

"Just help yourself, Bessie," he said. "Take all you want. Run your hand in the poke and eat until you is full. Dude, there, might hog it all if you don't take care of your own wants."

Jeeter was feeling fine. It was the first time since he could remember that he had been to Augusta and could get something to eat when he wanted it. He smiled at Bessie and Dude, and waved to people passing along the street. When a woman passed, he took off his hat and bowed.

"Augusta is a fine place," he said. "All these people here is just like us. They is rich, but that don't make no difference to me. I like everybody now."

"Where is we going now?" Bessie said.

"There's a place to sleep right up above the store," Jeeter said. "Supposing we sleep in there to-night, and then to-morrow morning sell the wood—ain't that what we ought to do?"

Dude liked the suggestion, but Bessie hesitated. It looked to her as if it might cost a lot of money to spend the night in the hotel.

"Maybe it will cost too much," she said. "You go upstairs and see how much it costs."

143

Jeeter stuffed another handful of crackers and cheese in his mouth, and went up the flight of stairs where the hotel was. There was a small sign over the door, dimly lighted, which said it was a hotel.

He came back in less than five minutes.

"They'll let us stay for fifty cents apiece," he said. "They is pretty much crowded, and there ain't but one room vacant, but we can stay if we wants to. I sure do, don't you, Bessie? I ain't never stayed all night in a hotel before."

Bessie by that time had set her heart on spending a night in a hotel in the city, and she was ready to go up the stairs when Jeeter said it would cost fifty cents for each of them.

"Now you hold on tight to that money, Jeeter," she said. "That's a heap of money to lose. You don't want to let it get away from you."

They walked up the narrow stairway and found themselves in a small, dusty room. It was the lobby. Half a dozen straight-back chairs and a table were in the dimly lighted room. The man who ran the hotel took them to the table and told them to sign their names on the register. Jeeter told him they would have to make their marks.

"What's your name?" he asked.

"Jeeter."

"Jeeter what?"

"Jeeter Lester, from out near Fuller."

"What's the boy's name?"

"Dude's name is Dude, the same as mine."

"Dude Lester?"

"That's right."

"And what's her name?" he asked, looking up at Bessie.

Bessie smiled at him, and he looked at her legs. She hunched her left shoulder forward and hung her head downward. He looked her over again.

"Her name is Mrs. Dude," Jeeter said.

The man looked at Dude and then at Bessie, and smiled. He was holding the pen for them to touch while he made the cross-marks opposite their names.

Jeeter gave him the money, and they were taken up another stairway to the third floor. The halls were dark, and the rooms shadowy and unventilated. He opened a door and told them to walk in.

"Is this where we sleep?" Jeeter asked him.

"This is the place. It's the only room I got left, too. We're pretty full to-night."

"This sure is a fine place," Jeeter said. "I didn't know hotels was such fine places before. I wish Lov was here to see me now."

There was only one bed in the room; it was large, flat, and high off the floor.

"I reckon we can crowd in the bed some way," Jeeter said. "I'll sleep in the middle."

"There's plenty of room for all of you," the man said, "but maybe I can find another bed for one of you."

He went out and shut the door.

Jeeter sat down on the bed and unlaced his brogans. The dusty shoes fell with heavy thuds on the bare floor. Dude sat in the chair and looked at the room, the walls, and the ceiling. The yellow plaster had dropped off in many places, and more hung loose, ready to fall the next time there was a vibration.

"We might as well go to bed," Jeeter said. "Ain't no sense in sitting up."

He hung his black felt hat on the bed-post and lay down. Bessie was standing before the wash-stand mirror taking down her hair.

"Ada ought to see me now," Jeeter said. "I ain't never slept the night in a hotel in all my days. I bet Ada won't believe I'm telling the truth when I tell her."

"You ain't got no business sleeping in bed with me and Bessie," Dude said. "You ought to get out on the floor."

145

"Now, Dude, you wouldn't begrudge me one night's sleeping, would you? Why, Bessie, there, is all willing, ain't you, Bessie?"

"You hush your mouth, Jeeter!" she said. "You make me feel so foolish when you say that!"

"It's only me and you, Dude," he said. "It's not like it was somebody else. I been wanting to sleep with you and Bessie for the longest time."

Some one knocked on the door and, before they could answer it, the man walked in.

"What did you say your name was?" he asked Bessie.

He walked over to the washstand where she stood, and waited close beside her.

"Mrs. Dude ———" Jeeter said. "I told you that already once."

"I know—but what's her first name? You know what I mean—her girl's name."

Bessie put her dress over herself before she told him.

"Bessie," she said. "What do you want to know that for?"

"That's all right, Bessie," he said. "That's all I wanted to know."

He went out and shut the door.

"These city folks has got the queerest ways," Jeeter said. "You don't never know what they is going to ask you next."

Dude took off his shoes and coat and waited for Bessie to get into bed. She had sat down on the floor to take off her shoes and stockings.

Jeeter sat up in bed and waited for her to finish. A door nearby was slammed so hard that pieces of yellow plaster dropped off the ceiling to the bed and floor.

Suddenly some one knocked on the door again, and it was opened immediately. This time it was a man whom they had not seen before.

"Come on down the hall, Bessie," he said.

He waited outside until Bessie got up from the floor and went to the door.

"Me?" she said. "What you want with me?"

"Come on down to this other room, Bessie. It's too crowded up here."

"They must have found another bed for us," Jeeter said. "I reckon they found out that there was more beds empty than they thought there was."

He and Dude watched Bessie gather up her clothes and leave the room. She carried her dress, shoes, and stockings in one hand, and her hat in the other. After the door was closed, the building became quiet again.

"These city people has queer ways, don't they, Dude?" Jeeter said, turning over and closing his eyes. "They ain't like us folks out around Fuller."

"Why didn't you go to the other bed?" Dude said. "Why did the man tell Bessie to go?"

"You never can tell about the queer ways of city folks, Dude. They do the durndest things sometimes."

They both lay awake for the next half hour, but neither of them said anything. The light was still burning, but they did not try to turn it off.

A board in the hall floor squeaked, and Bessie came in carrying her clothes in her hands.

"Don't you like the place they provided you with in the other room?" Jeeter asked, sitting up. "What made you come back, Bessie?"

"I reckon I must have got in the wrong bed by mistake or something," she said. "Somebody else was in it."

Dude rubbed his eyes in the glare of the electric light, and looked at Bessie.

"Bessie is sure a pretty woman preacher, ain't she?" Jeeter said, looking at her.

"I didn't have time to dress again," she said. "I had to leave right away, and there wasn't no time to put my clothes on."

"That man ought to know what he was doing at the start. Ain't no sense in making people change beds all night long. He ought to let folks stay in one bed all the time and let us sleep some."

"Men sure is queer in a hotel," Bessie said. "They say the queerest things and do the queerest things I ever saw. I'm sure glad we stayed here, because I been having a good time to-night. It ain't like it is out on the tobacco road."

There was a tapping on the door again, and a man opened it. He looked at Bessie, and beckoned her to the door.

"Come here, Bessie," he said, "there's a room down at the other end of the hall for you."

He waited outside the partly opened door.

"I went to one room just a little while ago, and there was a man in the bed."

"Well, that's all right. Down at this other room is another bed for you. Come on, I'll go with you and show you how to get there."

"By God and by Jesus," Jeeter said. "I never heard of the likes of it in all my life. The men here is going to wear Bessie out, running her from one bed to another all night long. I don't reckon I'll ever come to this kind of hotel again. I can't get no peace and sleep."

Bessie picked up her clothes and went out. The door was closed, and they heard her and the man walking down the hall.

"I reckon she's fixed up this time so she won't have to change beds again," Jeeter said. "I can't stay awake no longer to find out."

Dude went to sleep, too, in a few minutes.

At daybreak, Jeeter was up and dressed, and Dude got up a few minutes later. They sat in the room for the next

148

half hour waiting for Bessie. At last Jeeter got up and went to the door and looked up the hall and down it.

"I reckon we'll have to go hunt Sister Bessie," he said. "Maybe she got lost and can't find this room. It was dark out there last night, and things look different in the daytime up here in the city."

They opened the door and walked to the end of the hall. All the doors were closed, and Jeeter did not know which one to open. The first two he opened were not occupied, but the next one was. He turned the knob and went inside. There were two people asleep in the bed, but the woman was not Bessie. Jeeter backed out of the room and closed the door. Dude tried the next room. The door of that one was unlocked, too, and Jeeter had to go across the room and look at the woman's face before he was satisfied she was not Bessie. In the other rooms they entered they failed to find Bessie, and Jeeter did not know what to do. The last room they entered had only a single bed and he was about to close the door, when the girl opened her eyes and sat up. Jeeter stood looking at her, not knowing what else to do. When the girl was fully awake, she smiled and called Jeeter to her.

"What you want?" he said.

"Why did you come in here?" she said.

"I'm looking for Bessie, and I reckon I'd better go hunt for her some more. I'm liable to disgrace myself if I stay here looking at you."

She called Jeeter again, but he turned his back and ran out of the room. Dude caught up with his father.

"By God and by Jesus, Dude," Jeeter said. "I never saw so many pretty girls and women in all my days. This hotel is just jammed with them. I'd sure lose my religion if I stayed here much longer. I've got to get out in the street right now."

At the foot of the stairway they saw the man who had

rented them the room the night before. He was reading the morning paper.

"We're ready to leave now," Jeeter said, "but we can't find Sister Bessie."

"The woman who came in with you last night?"

"She's the one. Sister Bessie, her name is."

"I'll get her," he said, and started up the stairs. "What's wrong with her nose? I didn't notice it last night, but I saw it this morning. It gives me the creeps to look at it."

"She was born like that," Jeeter said. "Bessie ain't much to look at in the face, but she's a right smart piece to live with. Dude, here, he knows, because he's married to her."

"She's got the ungodliest-looking nose I ever saw," the man said, going up the stairs. "I hope I never get fooled like that again in the dark."

In about five minutes both he and Bessie came down the stairs. The man was in front and Bessie behind.

Out in the street, where they had left the car, Jeeter found the bag of crackers and cheese, and he began eating them hungrily. Dude took a handful of crackers and put them into his mouth. A few doors away was a store with a Coca-Cola sign on it, and all of them went in and got a drink.

"You don't look like you slept none too much last night," Jeeter said. "Couldn't you go to sleep, Bessie?"

She yawned and rubbed her face with the palms of her hands. She had dressed hurriedly, and had not combed her hair. It hung matted and stringy over her face.

"I reckon the hotel was pretty full last night," she said. "Every once in a while somebody came and called me to another room. Every room I went to there was somebody sleeping in the bed. Looked like nobody knowed where my bed was. They was always telling me to sleep in a new one. I didn't sleep none, except about an hour just a while ago. There sure is a lot of men staying there."

Jeeter led them outside the store and they got into the automobile and drove off towards the residential part of the city. Bessie yawned, and tried to take a nap on the front seat.

Selling the load of blackjack was no easier than it had been the afternoon before. Nobody wanted to buy wood, at least not the kind Jeeter had for sale.

By three o'clock that afternoon all of them were thoroughly tired of trying to find somebody to take the wood.

Sister Bessie wanted to go back home, and so did Jeeter. Bessie was sleepy and tired. Jeeter began swearing every time he saw a man walking along the street. His opinion of the citizens of Augusta was even less than it had been before he started the trip. He cursed every dollar in the city.

Dude was anxious to go back home, because he would have the opportunity of blowing the horn when they went around the long curves on the highway.

Bessie bought the gasoline and Jeeter paid for it out of the money they had left. No trouble with the engine developed, and they sailed along at a fast rate of speed for nearly ten miles.

"Let's stop a minute," Jeeter said.

Dude stopped the car without question and they all got out. Jeeter began untying the plow-lines and untwisting the baling wire around the load of blackjack.

"What you going to do now?" Bessie asked him, watching him begin throwing off the sticks.

"I'm going to throw off the whole durn load and set fire to it," he said. "It's bad luck to carry something to town to sell and then tote it back home. It ain't a safe thing to do, to take it back home. I'm going to pitch it all off."

Dude and Bessie helped him, and in a few minutes the blackjack was piled in the ditch beside the road.

"And I ain't going to let nobody else have the use of it, neither," he said. "If the rich people in Augusta won't

151

buy my wood, I ain't going to let it lay here so they can come out and take it off for nothing."

He gathered a handful of dead leaves, thrust them under the pile, and struck a match to them. The leaves blazed up, and a coil of smoke boiled into the air. Jeeter fanned the blaze with his hat and waited for the wood to catch on fire and burn.

"That was an unlucky trip to Augusta," he said. "I don't know when I've ever had such luck befall me before. All the other times I've been able to sell my wood for something, if it was only a quarter or so. But this time nobody wanted it for nothing, seems like."

"I want to go back some time and spend another night at that hotel," Bessie said, giggling. "I had the best time last night. It made me feel good, staying there. They sure know how to treat women real nice."

They waited for the blackjack to burn so they could leave for home. The leaves had burned to charred ashes, and the flame had gone out. The scrub oak would not catch on fire.

Jeeter scraped up a larger pile of leaves, set it on fire, and began tossing the sticks on it. The fire burned briskly for several minutes, and then went out under the weight of the green wood.

Jeeter stood looking at it, sadly. He did not know how to make it burn. Then Dude drew some gasoline from the tank and poured it on the pile. A great blaze sprang up ten or twelve feet into the air. Before long that too died down, leaving a pile of blackened sticks in the ditch.

"Well, I reckon that's all I can do to that damn-blasted blackjack," Jeeter said, getting into the car. "It looks like there ain't no way to get rid of the durn wood. It won't sell and it won't burn. I reckon the devil got into it."

They drove off in a swirl of yellow dust, and were soon nearing the tobacco road. Dude drove slowly through the deep white sand, blowing the horn all the way home.

152

CHAPTER XVII

THE next automobile trip Jeeter had planned after the return from Augusta was a journey over into Burke County to see Tom. From the things Jeeter had heard repeated by various men who had been in that section of the country, he knew Tom was a successful cross-tie contractor. Those men who had had business that took them close to the cross-tie camp came back to Fuller and told Jeeter that Tom was making more money than anybody else they knew. Jeeter was almost as proud of Tom as he was of Dude.

Very little else was known about Tom Lester. That was one of the reasons why Jeeter wanted to go over there. He wanted to find out how much money Tom was making, first of all, and then he wanted to ask Tom to give him a little money every week.

Bessie and Dude were not thinking of staying at home either while the new car was in running order. The trip to Augusta had not caused them to lose any of their enthusiasm for automobile travel any more than it had Jeeter. Springing the front axle, cracking the wind-shield, scarring the paint on the body, tearing holes in the upholstery, and parting with the spare tire and extra wheel were considered nothing more than the ordinary hazards of driving a car. The mashed front fender and broken rear spring had softened everybody's concern for the automobile. After their first accident, when Dude ran

153

into the back end of the two-horse wagon near McCoy and killed the colored man, anything else that happened to the car would not matter so very much, anyway.

Jeeter the next morning casually mentioned the fact that he would like very much to ride over to Burke County and see Tom.

Dude was filling the radiator at the time, and he stopped to hear what Bessie was going to say. She said nothing, and Dude picked up the bucket again and filled the radiator to overflowing. Jeeter walked away, waiting for Bessie to make up her mind. He went towards the rear of the house as if he were going to get out of sight until she had time to make up her mind definitely whether she would go or not. Jeeter did not go so far away that he could not keep his eye on the car. Bessie was liable to do most anything when his back was turned, and he did not want them to slip off and leave him.

"Jump in and let's go in a hurry, Dude," Bessie whispered excitedly, pushing him to the car. "Hurry, before your Pa sees us."

Jeeter was standing by the well, looking out across the broom-sedge, and he did not know they were getting ready to leave him.

When he heard Dude start the motor, he dashed for the automobile. By that time, Dude had got the gears engaged, and the car shot over the yard to the tobacco road.

He had swung the front wheels sharply, making a circle around the chinaberry trees, and he bumped over the ditch without slackening speed. They were away in a few short seconds, long before Jeeter could run to the road. He stood looking after them.

"Well, I never saw the likes of that," he said. "I don't know why they want to run off and leave me. I always treated Bessie fair and square. When a man gets old, folks seem to think that he don't care about riding around, and they go off and make him stay at home."

He stood watching them until the car was out of sight. Ada and Ellie May stood on the porch looking at the disappearing car. They had come to the door the moment they heard the car start. Both of them wanted to go somewhere, too; they had not been allowed inside the new car since it was bought.

Jeeter took a seat on the porch and sat down to wait for them to return. He was glum and silent the rest of the morning. When Ada told him to come into the kitchen at dinner time and eat some cheese and crackers, Jeeter did not move from his chair. Ada went back into the house without urging him to eat. There was so little food, she was glad he was not coming. The cheese and crackers that had been brought back from Augusta provided barely enough of a meal for one or two persons; and as he would not leave the porch, there would be more for her and Ellie May. It did not matter about the grandmother, because she was going to be given the cheese rinds and cracker crumbs that were left when they had finished. Jeeter always ate so fast that there was never time for anybody else to get his full share at any meal. Jeeter ate as if it were the last time he would ever taste food again.

Ada and Ellie May sat down to eat their meal, leaving Jeeter alone.

Late that afternoon when Bessie and Dude returned home, Jeeter was still waiting for them on the porch. He got up as they approached, and followed the car to its place beside the chimney. He was as angry as ever, but he had forgotten about it momentarily. He was anxious to know if they had found Tom.

"Did you see Tom?" he asked Bessie. "What was he doing? Did he send me some money?"

Ada came out to listen. The grandmother took her accustomed position behind a chinaberry tree, looking and listening. Ellie May came closer.

"Tom ain't at all like he used to be when I knowed him

155

better," Bessie said, shaking her head. "I don't know what's come over Tom."

"Why?" Jeeter asked. "What did he do—what did he say? Where's the money he sent me?"

"Tom didn't send no money. He don't appear to be aiming to help you none. He's a wicked man, Tom is."

"You ought to have taken me along, Bessie," Jeeter said. "I know Tom better than I do my own self. He was my special boy all along. Me and Tom got along all right together. The other children was always fighting with me, looks like now. But Tom never did. He was a fine boy when he was growing up."

Bessie listened to Jeeter talk, but she did not want to stop and argue about going off and leaving him at home. It was all over now. The trip was finished, and they were back.

"Why didn't you let me go along and see Tom?" he said.

"Tom works about a hundred ox," Dude said. He was very much impressed by the large number of oxen his brother worked at the cross-tie camp. "I didn't know there was that many ox in the whole country."

"When did Tom say he was coming over here to see me?" Jeeter asked.

"Tom said he wasn't never coming over here again," Dude said. "He told me to tell you he was going to stay where he was at."

"That sure don't sound like Tom talking," Jeeter said, shaking his head. "Maybe he has to work so hard all the time that he can't get off."

"Ain't that," Bessie said. "Tom said just what Dude told you. Tom said he ain't never coming over here again. He don't want to."

"That don't sound like Tom talking. Me and Tom used to get along first-rate concerning everything. Me and him never had no difficulties like I was always having

156

with my other children. They used to throw rocks at me and hit me over the head with sticks, but Tom never did. Tom was always a first-rate boy when I knowed him. Ain't no reason why he ought to change now, and be just like all the rest of them."

"I told him how bad off you was, and his Ma, too," Bessie said. "I told him you didn't have no meal or meat in the house half the time, and that you can't farm and raise a crop no more, and Tom says for you and Ada to go to the county poor-farm and stay."

"You made a mistake by telling Tom I wasn't going to farm no more. I'm going to raise me a big crop of cotton this year, if I can get hold of some seed-cotton and guano. The rest of what you told him is true and accurate, however. We is hungry pretty much of the time. That ain't no lie."

"Well, that's what he said, anyway. He told me to tell you and Ada to go to the county poor-farm and stay."

"That sure don't sound like Tom talking. Tom ain't never said nothing like that to me before. I can't see why he wants me and his Ma to go and live at the poor-farm. Looks like he would send me some money instead. I'm his daddy."

"I don't reckon that makes no difference to Tom now," she said. "He's looking after his own self."

"I wish I had my young age back again. I wouldn't beg of no man, not even my own son. But Tom ain't like he used to be. Looks like he would send me and his old Ma a little bit of money."

"Tom said to tell you to go to hell, too," Dude told Jeeter.

Bessie jumped forward, clutching Dude by the neck, and shook him until it looked as if his head would twist off and fall on the ground. She continued to shake him until he succeeded in escaping from her grasp.

"You shouldn't have told Jeeter that," she shouted at

157

Dude. "That's a wicked thing to say. I don't know nothing more sinful. The devil is trying to take you away from me so I can't make a preacher out of you."

"Christ Almighty!" he shouted at her. "You come near about killing me! I didn't say that—Tom said it. I was just telling him what Tom said. I didn't say it! You ought to keep off me. I didn't do nothing to you."

"Praise the Lord," Bessie said. "You ain't never going to make a preacher if you talk like that. I thought you said you was going to stop your cussing. Why don't you quit it?"

"I ain't going to say that no more," Dude pleaded. He remembered that the automobile belonged to her. "I wouldn't have said it that time if you hadn't hurt my neck shaking me so hard."

Jeeter walked around the automobile, trying to recover from the shock of hearing what they told him Tom had said. He could not believe that Tom had developed into a man who would tell his father to go to hell. He knew Tom must have changed a great deal since he knew him.

He stopped at the rear of the automobile and was looking at the rack where the spare tire and extra wheel had been, when he saw the great dent in the body. He stared at it until Dude and Bessie stopped talking.

"You won't be fit to preach a sermon next Sunday if you cuss like that," she was saying. "Good folks don't want to have God send them sermons by cussing preachers."

"I ain't going to say it no more. I ain't never going to cuss no more."

Jeeter motioned to them to come to the back of the car. He pointed to the dent in the body. The centre of it had been knocked in about ten or twelve inches, dividing the body into two almost equal halves.

"What done that?" he asked, still pointing.

"We was backing out from the cross-tie camp and ran smack into a big pine tree," Bessie said hesitantly. "I don't know what made it happen. Looks like everything has tried to ruin my new automobile. Ain't nothing like it was when I paid eight hundred dollars for it in Fuller the first of the week."

Dude ran his hands over the dent. The cracked paint dropped to the white sand. He tried to make the dent look smaller by rubbing it.

"It ain't hurt the running of it none, though, has it?" Jeeter said. "That's only the body smashed in. It runs good yet, don't it?"

"I reckon so," Bessie said, "but it does make a powerful lot of noise when it's running down hill—and up hill, too."

Ada came over and looked at the dent in the back of the car. She rubbed her hands over it until more of the cracked black paint dropped off and fell on the white sand at her feet.

"What does Tom look like now?" Ada asked Bessie. "I reckon he don't look like he used to, no more."

"He looks a lot like Jeeter," she said. "There ain't much resemblance in him and you."

"Humph!" Ada said. "There was a time when I'd declared it was the other way around."

Jeeter looked at Ada, and then at Bessie. He could not understand what Ada was talking about.

"What did Tom say when you told him you and Dude was married now?" Jeeter said.

"He didn't say nothing much. Looked to me like he didn't care one way or the other."

"Tom said she used to be a two-bit slut when he knowed her a long time back," Dude said. "He told it right to her, but she didn't say nothing. I reckon he knowed what he was talking about, because she didn't say it was a lie."

Sister Bessie grabbed Dude around the neck again and

159

shook him vigorously. Jeeter and Ada stood beside them watching. Ellie May had heard everything, but she had not come any closer.

Dude jerked away from Bessie more quickly than he had the first time. He was learning how to get away from her more easily.

"God damn you!" he shouted, striking at her face with his fist. "Why in hell don't you keep off me!"

"Now, Dude," Bessie pleaded tenderly, "you promised me you was not going to cuss no more. Good folks don't want to go and hear a Sunday sermon by a cussing preacher."

Dude shrugged his shoulders and walked away. He was getting tired of the way Bessie jumped on him and twisted his neck every time he said something she did not want to hear.

"When's Dude going to start being a preacher?" Jeeter asked her.

"He's going to preach a little short sermon next Sunday at the schoolhouse. I'm already telling him what to say when he preaches."

"Looks like to me he ought to know that himself," Jeeter said. "You don't have to tell him everything to do, do you? Don't he know nothing?"

"Well, he ain't familiar with preaching like I is. I tell him what to say and he learns to say it himself. It won't take him long to catch on and then I won't have to tell him nothing. My former husband told me what to say one Saturday night and I went to the schoolhouse the next afternoon and preached for almost three hours without stopping. It ain't hard to do after you catch on. Dude's already told me what he was going to preach about Sunday. He knows now what he's going to say when the time comes."

"What's he going to preach about Sunday?"

"About men wearing black shirts."

"Black shirts? What for?"

"You ask him. He knows."

"Black shirts ain't nothing to preach about, to my way of thinking. I ain't never heard of that before."

"You come to preaching at the schoolhouse Sunday afternoon and find out."

"Is he going to preach *for* black shirts, or *against* black shirts?"

"Against them."

"What for, Sister Bessie?"

"It ain't my place to tell you about Dude's preaching. That's for you to go to the schoolhouse and hear. Preachers don't want their secrets spread all over the country beforehand. Wouldn't nobody take the trouble to go and listen, if they did that."

"Maybe I don't know much about preaching, but I ain't never heard of nobody preaching about men wearing black shirts—against black shirts, at that. I ain't never seen a man wearing a black shirt, noway."

"Preachers has got to preach *against* something. It wouldn't do them no good to preach *for* everything. They got to be *against* something every time."

"I never looked at it that way before," Jeeter said, "but there might be a lot in what you say. Though, take for instance, God and heaven—you wouldn't preach *against* them, would you, Sister Bessie?"

"Good preachers don't preach about God and heaven, and things like that. They always preach *against* something, like hell and the devil. Them is things to be against. It wouldn't do a preacher no good to preach for God. He's got to preach against the devil and all wicked and sinful things. That's what the people like to hear about. They want to hear about the bad things."

"You sure is a convincing woman, Sister Bessie," he said. "God must be pretty proud of having a woman preacher like you. I don't know what He's going to think

161

about Dude, though. Specially when he starts preaching *against* men wearing black shirts. I ain't never seen a man wearing a black shirt, noway, and I don't believe there's such things in the country."

Jeeter bent over and rubbed his hands on the dent in the body of the car. He scraped the surface paint with his fingernails until most of it had peeled off and fallen on the ground.

"Stop doing that to my automobile," Bessie said. "Ain't you got no sense at all? You and Ada has near about got all the paint off of it already doing that."

"You wouldn't talk to me like that, would you, Bessie?" he asked. "I ain't hurting the automobile no more than it's already done."

"Well, you keep your hands off it, anyhow."

Jeeter slouched away and leaned against the corner of the house. He looked sharply at Bessie, saying nothing.

"I near about ruined my new automobile letting you fool with it," she said. "I ought to had better sense than to let you get near it. Hauling that load of blackjack to Augusta tore holes all in the back seat."

"You ain't going to take me riding in it none?" he asked, standing erectly by the house.

"No, sir! You ain't going to ride in my new automobile no more. That's why I wouldn't let you go with me to see Tom this morning. I don't want you around it no more, neither."

"By God and by Jesus, if that's what you're aiming to do, you can get off my land," he said, shifting his weight from one foot to the other and pulling at the rotten weatherboards behind him. "I ain't none too pleased to have you around, noway."

Bessie did not know what to say. She looked around for Dude, but he was not in sight.

"You're going to make me leave?"

162

"I done started doing it. I already told you to get off my land."

"It don't belong to you. It's Captain John's land. He owns it."

"It's the old Lester place. Captain John ain't got no more right to it than nobody else. Them rich people up there in Augusta come down here and take everything a man's got, but they can't take the land away from me. By God and by Jesus, my daddy owned it, and his daddy before him, and I ain't going to get off it while I'm alive. But durned if I can't run you off it—now git!"

"Me and Dude ain't got no place to go. The roof is all rotted away at my house."

"That don't make no difference to me. I don't care where you go, but you're going to get off this land. If you ain't going to let me ride in the new automobile when I wants to, you can't stay here. I'm tired looking at them two dirty holes in your durn nose, anyhow."

"You old son of a bitch, you!" she cried, running to him and scratching his face with her fingernails. "You're nothing but an old dirty son of a bitch, you is! I hope God sends you straight to hell and never lets you out again!"

Ada came running around the corner of the house when she heard the cries of Bessie. The sight of Jeeter's bleeding face threw her into a fit of uncontrollable anger. She hit at Bessie with her fists and kicked her with her feet.

Dude came running, too. He stood looking at the fight while all three of them were striking and scratching one another. Ellie May grinned from behind a chinaberry tree.

Bessie retreated. Both Ada and Jeeter were fighting her, and she was unable to strike back. She ran to the automobile and jumped in. Jeeter picked up a stick and hit her with it several times before Ada took it from him and began poking Bessie in the ribs with it. The sharp

163

point hurt her much more than Jeeter's blows on her head and shoulders had, and she screamed with pain.

Both Ellie May and the grandmother came out from behind the chinaberry trees and watched all that was taking place.

Dude jumped in and backed the car towards the road as fast as he could. His choice lay with Sister Bessie. He liked to drive an automobile too much to let hers get away from him on account of a little scrap like that.

Mother Lester, who had watched the fight from the start, ran across the yard to get behind another chinaberry tree where she could see from a better location everything that was happening. She had no more than reached a point midway between two chinaberry trees when the rear end of the automobile struck her, knocking her down and backing over her.

Bessie leaned out of the car, shaking her fists and making faces at Ada and Jeeter. They followed the automobile to the tobacco road.

"You old sons of bitches, you!" she yelled at them at the top of her high-pitched voice. "All of you Lesters is dirty sons of bitches!"

Ada picked up a big rock and hurled it at the car as hard as she could. By that time, Bessie and Dude were several hundred feet away, and Ada's big stone fell short of the mark by three-fourths of the distance. She should have known she did not have the strength to throw rocks as large as that. It was almost as big as a stove-lid.

CHAPTER XVIII

AFTER the dust had settled on the road, Ada and Jeeter came back into the yard. Mother Lester still lay there, her face mashed on the hard white sand. From the corner of the house, Ellie May looked at what had happened.

"Is she dead yet?" Ada asked, looking at Jeeter. "She don't make no sound and she don't move. I don't reckon she could stay alive with her face all mashed like that."

Jeeter did not answer her. He was too busy thinking of his hatred for Bessie to bother with anything else. He took another look at the grandmother and walked across the yard and around to the back of the house. Ada went to the porch and stood there looking back at Mother Lester several minutes, then she walked inside and shut the door.

Mother Lester tried to turn over so she could get up and go into the house. She could not move either her arms or her legs without unbearable pain, and her head felt as if it had been cracked open. The automobile had struck her with such force that she did not know what had hit her. Both of the left wheels had rolled over her, one of them across her back and the other on her head. She had not known what had happened. More than anything else she wanted to get up and lie down on her bed. She struggled with a final effort to raise her head and shoulders from the hard sand, and she managed to turn over. After that she lay motionless.

165

When he had finished getting a fresh drink of water at the well, Jeeter walked out into the broom-sedge, kicking the ground with the toes of his shoes to find out how dry it was. He believed the soil held just the right amount of moisture needed for plowing, but he wanted to be sure of it, because he was confident that he could borrow a mule somewhere and begin plowing and planting early the following week.

While he walked around in the waist-high broom-sedge, Lov was racing down the tobacco road, hatless and out of breath. Lov began shouting to Jeeter as soon as he reached the front yard, and Jeeter ran out of the sedge to meet him and find out what the trouble was.

Lov was dressed in his dirty black overalls, the pair he wore at the chute when he shovelled coal into the scoops. His hat had blown off when he started running to Jeeter's, and he had not waited to go back and pick it up. Lov's fiery red hair stood almost straight up; ordinarily, it was falling down over his forehead and getting into his eyes.

He saw the old grandmother lying in the yard and he slowed down to look at her, but he did not linger there. He ran until he was face to face with Jeeter.

"What you doing down here at this time of day, Lov?" Jeeter said. "Why ain't you working at the chute?"

Lov did not speak for several minutes. He had to wait until he could regain his breath. He sat on the ground, and Jeeter squatted on his heels beside him.

They were not far from the well. Ellie May was standing beside the stand drinking from the bucket when Lov reached Jeeter, but she did not run away immediately. She waited until Lov sat down, so she could hear what he had to tell Jeeter.

"What's the matter, Lov?" Jeeter asked. "What happened down at the chute that made you run here so fast?"

"Pearl—Pearl—she run off!"

"Run where to?" Jeeter asked calmly, disappointed because it was not something of more interest to him. "Where'd Pearl run to, Lov?"

"She's gone to Augusta!"

"Gone to Augusta!" Jeeter said, straightening up. "I thought maybe she just went off in the woods somewhere for a spell, like she was always doing. Reckon what she run off to Augusta for?"

"I don't know," Lov said, "but I reckon she just up and went. I don't know what else she done it for. I didn't hurt her none this morning. I didn't do nothing to her, except throw her down on the bed. She got loose from me, and I ain't seen her since."

"What was you trying to do to her?"

"Nothing. I was only going to tie her up with some plow-lines to see if I could do it. I figured she'd have to stay in the bed if I tied her there. I was going to turn her loose pretty soon."

"How you know she's run off to Augusta? Maybe she just went off in the woods somewhere again. Did she tell you she was going to run off to Augusta?"

"She didn't say nothing to me."

"Then what makes you think she went up there, instead of going off in the woods somewhere?"

"I didn't even know she was running off up there till Jones Peabody came by the chute and told me he met her up near Augusta when he was coming back to Fuller with an empty lumber truck. He said he stopped and asked her where she was going to, and if I knowed she'd left home, but she wouldn't talk to him. He said she looked like she was near about scared to death. He came and told me about it the first thing. He said he knowed I wouldn't know about it."

"Pearl, she was just like Lizzie Belle. Lizzie Belle up and went to Augusta just like that!" He snapped his fingers, jerking his head to one side. "I didn't know nothing

167

about it till I seen her up there on the street once. I asked her what made her run off without saying nothing to her Ma and me about it, but she wouldn't talk none. I thought all the time that she was staying out in the woods somewhere for a while, but I knowed it was Lizzie Belle the first time I looked at her. She had on some stylish clothes and a hat, but they didn't fool me. I knowed it was Lizzie Belle, even if she wouldn't talk to me. She was working in a cotton mill across the river from there, all that time. I knowed then why she up and went there, because Ada told me. Ada said Lizzie Belle wanted to have some stylish clothes and a hat to wear, and she run off up there to work in a cotton mill so she could get them kind of things herself."

"Pearl never said nothing to me about wanting a stylish dress and a hat," Lov said. "I make a dollar a day at the chute, and I could have bought her a dress and a hat if she had told me she wanted them. But Pearl never said nothing to me—she never said nothing to nobody. She slept on that durn pallet on the floor and wouldn't answer my requests when I told her to do something I wanted done."

"I reckon about the best thing you can do, Lov, is to let her be. She wasn't satisfied living down here on the tobacco road, and if you was to bring her back, she'd run off again twice as quick. She's just like Lizzie Belle and Clara and the other gals. I can't recall all of their names right now, but it was every durn one of them, anyhow. They all wanted some stylish clothes. They wasn't satisfied with the pretty calico and gingham their Ma sewed for them. Well, Ada ain't satisfied neither, but she can't do nothing about it. That's how the gals took after their Ma. I sort of broke Ada of wanting to go off and do that. She don't talk no more about buying of stylish clothes and a hat, excepting a dress to die in and be buried in. She talks about getting a stylish dress to die in, but she ain't going to get it, and she knows she ain't. She'll die and be buried in the ground wearing that yellow calico she's got on now. I broke Ada of wanting to run off, but them gals was more than I could take care of. There was too durn many of them for only one man to break. They just up and went."

"Maybe she'll come back," Lov said. "Reckon she'll come back, Jeeter?"

"Who—Pearl? Well, I wouldn't put no trust in it. Lizzie Belle went off and she ain't never come back. None of the other gals came back, neither."

"I sort of hate to lose her, for some reason or another. She was a pretty little girl—all them long yellow curls hanging down her back always made me hate the time when she'd grow up and be old. I used to sit on the porch and watch her through the window when she was combing and brushing her hair in the bedroom ———"

"That sure ain't no lie," Jeeter said. "Pearl had the prettiest yellow hair of any gal I ever saw. It was a plumb shame that she was so bad about wanting to stay by herself all the time, because I used to want to have her around me. I wish Ada had been that pretty. Even when Ada was a young gal, she was that durn ugly it was a sin. I ain't never seen an uglier woman in the whole country, unless it's that durn woman preacher Bessie. Them two dirty holes in her face don't do a man no good to look at."

"Pearl always took a long time to fix herself up, woman-like. I used to want to tell her there wasn't no other girl in the whole country who was nowhere as pretty as she was, but she wouldn't listen to me. And I lived with her so long I sort of got used to seeing her every day, and I don't know what I'm going to do now when she's gone to Augusta to stay. I'll miss them long yellow curls hanging down her back, and that pretty face of hers, too. Aside from that, I don't know of a prettier sight to see than to look in her pale blue eyes early in the morning before the sun got up so high it threw too much light in them. Early in the morning they was the prettiest things a man could ever want to look at. But they was pretty any time of the day, and sometimes I used to sit and shake all over, for wanting to squeeze her so hard. I don't reckon I'll ever forget how pretty her eyes was early in the morning just when the sun was rising."

"Maybe you would like to take Ellie May down to your house, Lov?" Jeeter suggested. "She ain't got a man, and it looks like she ain't never going to get one, unless you take a fancy to her. You and Ellie May was hugging and rubbing of the other the first of the week, around at the front of the house. Maybe you would want to do that some more?"

"Reckon if I was to go up to Augusta and find her, she would let me bring her back home to stay?" Lov said. "Reckon she would, Jeeter?"

"Who—Pearl?" Jeeter said. "No, I wouldn't recommend that. You'll lose your time down there at the chute while you was looking for her, and it's like I said at the start. Pearl is just like Lizzie Belle and Clara and all the rest of the gals. They was plumb crazy for getting stylish clothes. None of them gals of mine liked to wear the calico and gingham Ada sewed."

"But Pearl—she might get hurt up there in Augusta ———"

"Lizzie Belle and Clara took care of themselves all right, didn't they? They didn't get hurt none. Now, as I was saying about Ellie May. You can take her to your house, Lov. Ellie May would be crazy about going down there to stay all the time. She wouldn't be never getting down on no durn pallet on the floor, neither."

"Seeing them long yellow curls hanging down her back used to make me cry sometimes. I'd look at her pretty hair and eyes so long that I thought I'd go crazy if I didn't touch her and see deep down into her eyes. But she wouldn't never let me come close to her, and that's what made the tears fall out of my eyes, I reckon. I been the lonesomest man in the whole country, for the longest time. Pearl was so pretty it was a sin for her to do like she done."

"Ellie May's got to get a man somewhere. She can't stay here all the time. When me and Ada's dead and gone, there won't be nobody to watch after her. If she stayed here at the house by herself the niggers would haul off and come here by the dozens. The niggers would get her in no time, if she was here by herself."

"The last pretty I got for Pearl was some green beads on a long string. I gave them to her and she put them around her neck, and I swear to God if it didn't make her the prettiest little girl I ever saw or heard about in the whole country."

"If you want to take Ellie May with you now, I'll tell her to wash herself up and get ready to go," Jeeter said.

"I might take Ellie May for a while, and I might not. I don't know what I'm going to do about Pearl, yet. I wish I could get her to come back."

"Ellie May's got ———"

"Ellie May's got that ugly-looking face," Lov said. "I don't know as how I would want to look at it all the time."

"You would sort of get used to it, slow-like," Jeeter said. "It don't bother me none now. I got used to looking at the slit and I don't notice it no more."

Lov stood up and leaned against the well. He was silent for a long time, looking out over the tall brown broom-sedge. Jeeter watched him, and whittled on a little stick with his pocketknife.

Ellie May was behind another chinaberry tree then. She had moved from one to another while Lov and Jeeter were busy talking. She had at last come closer so she could hear what was being said.

Presently Lov turned around and looked at Ellie May.

She jerked her head behind the chinaberry tree before he could see her face.

"I've got to be going back to the chute," he said. "That afternoon freight will be coming along pretty soon now, and it always empties all the scoops. I got to get back and fill them up before the passenger comes. They raise hell about the scoops being empty, because that makes the train have to wait until I can load them up."

He and Jeeter went around the house to the front yard. Neither of them had thought of Mother Lester again until they saw her lying on the sand. She was procumbent, and her face was mashed on the ground, but she had moved several feet closer to the house.

"What's wrong with her?" Lov said.

"Dude and Bessie backed the new automobile over her when they left. They was trying to get away before I could hit Bessie again, and they ran over her. I got it in good and heavy for that woman preacher now. I ain't letting her set foot on my land another time. She treated me bad about riding in the new automobile. She wouldn't let me go riding with her at all."

Lov walked over to where the old grandmother lay on the hard white sand. She had stopped bleeding, and she made no sound.

"Looks like she's dead," he said. "Is she dead, Jeeter?"

Jeeter looked down and moved one of her arms with his foot.

"She ain't stiff yet, but I don't reckon she'll live. You help me tote her out in the field and I'll dig a ditch to put her in."

They carried the body by the hands and feet, and put it down in the broom-sedge. Jeeter went to get a shovel from behind the corn-crib.

"You think that over what I said about Ellie May," Jeeter said. "I'll send her down to your house in time to cook your supper to-night. Ellie May won't treat you bad

172

like Pearl done. Ellie May won't sleep on no durn pallet on the floor."

Lov started back down the tobacco road towards the coal chute. He shuffled his feet along the road, filling his shoes with sand. He did not look back.

Jeeter went out into the field with the shovel and began digging a grave to put his mother in. He dug in the earth for ten or fifteen minutes, and then called Ellie May. She had been standing in the yard behind a chinaberry tree waiting for Jeeter to tell her to go to Lov's.

"You wash yourself and go down to Lov's house and fix up for him," he told her, leaning wearily on the shovel handle. "He'll be coming home for supper to-night, and you cook him what he tells you."

Ellie May dashed into the house before Jeeter could finish giving her his instructions. She could not wait any longer.

He dug some more earth out of the ground, making the ditch a little longer.

Ellie May came out of the house in less than five minutes, running towards the road. Jeeter threw down the shovel and ran after her, calling her.

"You come back here in the morning after Lov goes to work and bring some victuals with you, do you hear?" he shouted. "Lov makes a dollar a day at the chute, and he's got rations for a lot of victuals. Me and your Ma ain't got nothing up here. We get pretty hungry sometimes. You remember that."

Ellie May had run all the way across the yard and was racing down the middle of the tobacco road as fast as she could. Before Jeeter could say anything else to her, she was a hundred yards away. He had wanted to tell her to bring him a pair of Lov's overalls too, the next morning when she brought the cooked food. She looked as if she was in such a great hurry to reach Lov's house that he let her go. She could make another trip the next day with the overalls.

173

CHAPTER XIX

THE time for spring plowing was over. Throughout the last two weeks of February the weather had been dry and the ground crumbly; there had been no finer season for plowing and planting in six or seven years. Usually at that time rains came every few days and kept the earth continually wet and soggy; but this year the season had begun in the middle of February with clearing skies, and a gentle breeze had been drying the moisture in the ground ever since the winter rains had stopped.

Farmers around Fuller who were undertaking to raise a crop of cotton this year had finished their plowing by the end of the month. With such an early start, there seemed to be no reason why, with plenty of hot weather during the growing season, the land should not yield a bale of cotton to the acre that fall. All farmers would put in as much guano as they could buy, and there was no limit to the number of pounds of cotton an acre would yield if fertilizer could be bought and used with a free hand. A bale to the acre was the goal of every cotton farmer around Fuller; but the boll-weevil and hard summer rains generally cut the crop in half. And on the other hand, if it was a good year for the raising of cotton, the price would probably drop lower than it had before. Not many men felt like working all year for six- or seven-cent cotton in the fall.

Jeeter had lived through the season for burning broom-sedge and pine woods, and through the time for spring plowing, without having done either. It was still not too late to begin, but Jeeter did not have a mule, and he did not have the credit to purchase seed-cotton and guano at the stores. Up until this year, he had lived in the hope that something would happen at the last moment to provide a mule and credit, but now it seemed to him that there was no use hoping for anything any more. He could still look forward to the following year when he could perhaps raise a crop of cotton, but it was an anticipation not so keen as it once had been. He had felt himself sink lower and lower, his condition fall further and further, year after year, until now his trust in God and the land was at the stage where further disappointment might easily cause him to lose his mind and reason. He still could not understand why he had nothing, and would never have anything, and there was no one who knew and who could tell him. It was the unsolved mystery of his life.

But, even if he could not raise a crop that year, he could at least make all preparations for one. He could burn over the broom-sedge and the groves of blackjack and the fields of young pine seedlings. He could have the land ready for plowing in case something happened that would let him plant a crop of cotton. He would have the land ready, in case ———

It was late afternoon on the first of March. He walked across the old cotton field through the waist-high broom-sedge towards the blackjack grove at the rear of the house; he kicked at the crumbly earth lying exposed between the tufts of sedge, thinking there was still time in which to arrange for credit at the stores in Fuller. He knew the time for burning and plowing had ended the day before, but there still lingered in the warm March air something of the new season. The smell of freshly

175

turned earth and the odor of pine and sedge-smoke hovered over the land even after burning and plowing was done. He breathed deeply of it, filling his body with the invigorating aroma.

"Maybe God will send some way to allow the growing of a crop," he said. "He puts the land here, and the sun and rain—He ought to furnish the seed and the guano, somehow or other."

Jeeter firmly believed that something would happen so he would be able to keep his body and soul alive. He still had hope left.

The late afternoon sun was still warm, and the air was balmy. There had been no cold nights for almost a week. People could sit on their front porches in the evening now without feeling the chill night air of February.

The breeze was blowing from the east. The white smoke of the broom-sedge fire coiled upward and was carried away towards the west, away from Jeeter's view of the house and tobacco road. He stood watching it burn slowly away from him, and at the fire eating along the ground under the brown broom-sedge. There were several hundred acres of the land to burn; the fields that had not been cultivated, some of them for ten or fifteen years, were matted with the dry grass. Beyond the fields lay the woods of yellow pine and blackjack. The fire would probably blaze and smoulder three or four days before it would burn itself out and die along the shores of the creeks farther away.

"If Tom and some of the older boys was here, maybe they could help get some seed-cotton and guano somehow," he said. "I know where I might could borrow a mule, if I had the seed-cotton and guano to plant. But a mule ain't no good without the rest of things. Wouldn't nothing grow in the new rows except broom-sedge and blackjack sprouts."

He walked back to the house, to sit on the back steps a

176

while before bed-time and watch the long line of yellow fire in the sedge.

It was long after dark before he got up and went into the house. From the rear bedroom window where he stood taking off his heavy shoes, Jeeter watched with fascination the distant fire that had melted into a vivid red with the fall of darkness. Some of the fire had gone far over the hills, and all that could be seen of it was the dull orange glow in the sky above it. Other sections of it had circled around the fields like cornered snakes, and burned on both sides of the house. In the centre, where he had stood that afternoon when he struck the match, there was a deep dark hole in the earth. The ground would remain black until it rained again.

He lay awake a long time after Ada was asleep. It was quiet in the house, now that there was no one else there to keep them company.

Jeeter tossed and turned, smelling the aroma of pine and broom-sedge smoke in the night air. With it came the strong odor of freshly turned earth somewhere a long way off. He looked straight up at the black ceiling, solemnly swearing to get up the next morning and borrow a mule. He was going to plow a patch to raise some cotton on, if he never did anything else as long as he lived.

He went to sleep then, his mind filled with thoughts of the land and its sweet odors, and with a new determination to stir the earth and cultivate plants of cotton.

The fire burned lustily through the night. It went farther and farther towards the west where the young pines grew, and it burned through the groves of blackjack, leaving the scrub-oak trees standing blackened and charred. They would not die, but the young pines would.

The dawn was beginning to break in the east, and the wind shifted to the north, blowing a final night breeze before daylight. The fire in the broom-sedge on each side of the house burst into renewed vigor in the path of the

177

wind, and it burned back towards the center where it had started. When it reached the point where the sedge ended at the rim of blackened ground, it would die out. In the meantime there were the fields on each side of the house to burn. After that, there would remain to be burned only the land far back in the woods and on the hills where the blue smoke and red flames climbed above the tree-tops.

Beside the house, the broom-sedge fire leapt higher in the early morning breeze. It came closer and closer to the house, and only a thin strip of sandy yard separated it from the building. If a brisk wind caught the fire at the moment when it was burning hardest, it would whirl the embers of grass against the house, under it, and onto the roof.

The moment when the sun came up, the wind caught the fire and sent it swirling through the dry grass. Torn by the wind, stems of flaming grass were showered on the house, some dying as they burned out, others leaving a glowing spark imbedded in the dry tinder-like shingles that had covered the house for fifty years or more. There were cracks in the roof where the more rotten shingles had been ripped and blown away by the strong autumnal winds, and in these the embers spread quickly.

Jeeter and Ada usually got up with the sun, and it was that time now. Neither of them came to the windows now, however, nor did either of them open the door. They were both asleep.

The fiery, red flaming roof was a whirling mass of showering embers in a short time. The dry tinder-like shingles, rotted by the autumn and winter rains and scorched by the searing spring and summer sun for two generations, blazed like coals in a forge. The whole roof was in flames in a few seconds, and after that it was only a matter of minutes until the rafters, dry and dripping with pine pitch, fell down upon the floor of the house and upon

178

the beds. Half an hour after the roof had first caught, the house was in black smoking ashes. Ada and Jeeter had not known what had happened.

Several near-by farmers had seen the smoke and flames as they were getting up at sun-rise. Most of them hurried along the tobacco road and across the fields to the Lester place with the intention of helping to save some of the furniture. They had not realized how fast the dry pitch-dripped house had burned to the ground, until they reached it.

There was a crowd of twenty or thirty men standing around the ashes when Lov and Ellie May reached the place, and when Bessie and Dude got there. There was nothing anybody could do then. There was nothing that could be saved. Jeeter's old automobile was a pile of rust-colored junk.

Some of the men took long blackjack poles and poked around in the mass of ashes, hoping to find the bodies and to take them out before they were burned any more, but the heat of the ashes drove every one back for a while.

"The Lord had a curse on this house," Bessie said. "He didn't want it to stand no longer. Praise the Lord!"

Nobody paid any attention to Bessie.

"Jeeter is better off now than he was," one of the farmers said. "He was near about starved to death half the time and he couldn't raise no crops. It looks to me like his children ought to have stayed at home and helped him run a farm."

Lov's first thought on seeing the smoking ashes was to remember Jeeter's prayerful plea about the care he wanted taken of his body when he died. Now it did not matter, because there was very little of it left.

After the coals had cooled, the men went into the ashes and carried out the two bodies and laid them down under the chinaberry tree beside the road. The tree's green limbs had been scorched, but it was too far away from the house to burn. The other chinaberry trees in the yard had been closer to the house, and they had burned almost as quickly as the house.

Preparations were begun at once to dig the grave. The men found two or three charred and broken-handled shovels and a pick behind the scorched and blistered corn-crib, and asked Lov where he wanted the grave dug. They decided to dig it in the blackjack grove, because if some one did decide to farm the land that year or the following ones, there would be no danger of the grave being plowed up so soon.

The men dug the grave, and carried the remains, stretched out on blackjack poles, to the grove. They were lowered into the ground. Some of the men asked Bessie to say a short prayer before the bodies were covered, but she refused to say anything for Jeeter or Ada. There was nothing, then, left to do but to throw the earth in and smooth the mounds with the back of the shovels.

Most of the farmers hurried back to their homes for breakfast. There was nothing else to be done.

Lov sat down by the lone chinaberry tree and looked at the blackened mass of ashes. Bessie and Dude stayed a while, too; they had to wait on Lov. Ellie May hovered in the distance, looking on, but never coming close enough to be noticed by Lov or the others.

"I reckon old Jeeter had the best thing happen to him," Lov said. "He was killing himself worrying all the time about the raising of a crop. That was all he wanted in this life—growing cotton was better than anything else to him. There ain't many more like him left, I reckon. Most of the people now don't care about nothing except getting a job in a cotton mill somewhere. But can't all of them work in the mills, and they'll have to stay here like Jeeter until they get taken away too. There ain't no sense in them raising crops. They can't make no money at it, not even a living. If they do make some cotton, somebody comes along and cheats them out of it. It looks like the Lord don't care about crops being raised no more like He used to, or He would be more helpful to the poor. He could make the rich people lend out their money, and stop holding it up. I can't figure out how they got hold of all the money in the county, anyhow. Looks like it ought to be spread out among everybody."

Dude poked around in the ashes looking for whatever he could find. There had been nothing of value in the house; but he liked to dig in the ashes and toss out the twisted tin kitchen dishes and china doorknobs. The charred and crusted iron casters of the wooden beds were there, and nails and screws; almost everything else in the house had been made of wood or cloth.

"Old Jeeter had one wish fulfilled," Lov said. "It wasn't exactly fulfilled, but it was taken care of, anyhow. He used to tell me he didn't want me to lock him up in the corn-crib and go off and leave him when he died. That's what happened to his daddy. When his daddy died, Jeeter and the men who were sitting up with the body locked it in the corn-crib at night while they rode to Fuller for tobacco and drinks. They put it in the crib so nothing would happen to it while they was gone. When they went to bury it the next day, a big crib rat jumped out of the box. It had gnawed into the coffin while it was shut up in the crib, and it had eaten all one side of the older Lester's face and neck. That was what Jeeter was afraid would happen to him, and he used to make me promise two or three times a day that I wouldn't lock him up in the crib when he died. There wasn't no use of him worrying so, because there ain't been no rats in the crib in many a year, except when they come back sometimes to look around and see if any corn has been put in it."

"I don't think the Lord took to Jeeter none too much," Sister Bessie said. "Jeeter must have been a powerful sinful man in his prime, because the Lord wasn't good to him like He is to me. The Lord knows us all like that. He knows when we're good and when the devil is in us."

"Well, it don't make no special difference now," Lov said. "Jeeter's dead and gone, and he won't be bothered no more by wanting to grow things in the ground. That's what he liked to do more than anything else, but somehow he never got a chance to do it much. Jeeter, he would lots rather grow a big crop of cotton than go to heaven."

"If he'd gone to Augusta and worked in the cotton mills like the rest of them done, he would have been all right. There ain't no money for a man like him farming all the time when he can't get no credit."

"I reckon Jeeter done right," Lov contended. "He was a man who liked to grow things in the ground. The mills ain't no place for a human who's got that in his bones. The mills is sort of like automobiles—they're all right to fool around in and have a good time in, but they don't offer no love like the ground does. The ground sort of looks out after the people who keeps their feet on it. When people stand on planks in buildings all the time, and walk around on hard streets, the ground sort of loses interest in the human."

Dude came out of the ashes, shaking the black flakes off his shoes and overalls. He sat on the ground and looked on silently. Ellie May still hovered in the distance, as if she were afraid to come any closer to the ashes of the house.

"Ada didn't get no stylish dress to die in, though," Lov said. "I sort of hoped she would, too. It's a pity about that, but it don't make no difference now. Her old dress was burned off of her in the fire, and she was buried just like God made her. Maybe that was better than having a stylish dress, after all. If she had died of age, or anything like that, she wouldn't have had no stylish dress, noway.

182

She would have had to be buried in the old one she had. It sort of worked out just right for her. She didn't know she didn't have a stylish dress to die in. It didn't make no difference if it was the right length or not."

No one mentioned the old grandmother, but Lov was glad she had been killed the day before. He did not feel that it would have been right to bury her body in the same grave with Jeeter and Ada, or even in the same field. They had hated her so much that it would have been taking advantage of her death to put Mother Lester's body next to theirs. She had lived so long in the house with Jeeter and Ada that she had been considered nothing more than a door-jamb or a length of weather-boarding. But it could be said about her, Lov thought to himself, that she never complained of the treatment she received. Even when she was hungry, or sick, no word had passed her lips. She had lived so long with Ada and Jeeter that she had believed it was useless to try to protest. If she had said anything, Jeeter or Ada would have knocked her down.

Dude was the first to get into the automobile, and Sister Bessie soon followed. They waited for Lov to get in so they could go back to their house and cook breakfast. After he was in, Ellie May came and sat down beside him on the back seat. Dude steered the car out of the yard, and turned down the tobacco road towards the blackened coal chute and the muddy red river.

Almost immediately, Dude began blowing the horn.

When they were going over the first sand hill, Lov looked back through the rear curtain and saw the Lester place. The tall brick chimney standing blackened and tomb-like in the early morning sunlight was the only thing that he could see.

Dude took his hand off the horn-button and looked back at Lov.

"I reckon I'll get me a mule somewhere and some seed-

183

cotton and guano, and grow me a crop of cotton this year," Dude said. "It feels to me like it's going to be a good year for cotton. Maybe I could grow me a bale to the acre, like Pa was always talking about doing."